Tinsel in a Tangle

TINSEL IN A TANGLE

FAIRY TALES OF A TRAILER PARK QUEEN, BOOK 2

KIMBRA SWAIN

CRIMSON SUN
PRESS

Kimbra Swain
Tinsel in a Tangle: Fairy Tales of a Trailer Park Queen, Book 2
©2017, Kimbra Swain / Crimson Sun Press, LLC
kimbraswain@gmail.com

ISBN: 978-0-9993609-2-7

Cover art by Hampton Lamoureux @ TS95 Studios https://www.ts95studios.com
Formatting by Serendipity Formats:
https://serendipityformats.wixsite.com/formats
Editing by Carol Tietsworth: https://www.facebook.com/Editing-by-Carol-Tietsworth-328303247526664/

Contorting my head sideways, I hoped to instruct my dear bard on the shortcomings of his current task. "Levi, it's crooked."

"No, it isn't," he complained.

"Yes, it is, honey," Kady said, sitting beside me.

"It's not fair that there are two of you now to gang up on me," he whined.

"You have no holiday spirit," I said giggling at him. "Dublin, the whole tree is crooked, not just the star."

Christmas back in the Otherworld was celebrated as Yule around the winter solstice. The longest day of the year. It symbolized the darkness giving into the light. I never really liked the celebration, plus I'd spent my entire life in the human realm avoiding the darkness. Especially that darkness within myself. The celebration always reminded me that no matter what the orbit of the sun, the darkness inside of me continued to fester. However, the human celebrations of Christmas involved lots of lights, decorations, and family. The celebration also switched dates over the years as humans tinkered with the calendar. I never had much family until recently, but I loved decorating a Christmas tree, stringing lights and baking cookies. In fact, Christmas was why I learned to cook.

When I moved into my first trailer park, an older woman by the name of Sharolyn brought me into her family as one of her own. She loaned me her recipes teaching me all the shortcuts and secrets to really good food. I'd spent ages in the human realm, and what little contact I had with humans was generally sexual. Until Miss Sharolyn. Christmas reminded me of her and the family I didn't have.

But, I finally *had* a family. A misfit one of sorts, but they were mine. I watched Levi trying to set the tree straight and the cold recesses of my heart melted into the warmth of actually belonging somewhere. Home. Family. Christmas.

"I don't know why we are putting a star on it, because it's supposed to be an angel," he continued to moan.

"The last thing an angel needs is a piece of evergreen up his butt," I laughed. Kady laughed too, but Nestor Gwinn, the bar owner and my grandfather, huffed behind us. "What's wrong, Nestor?"

"Grace, have you ever met an angel?" he asked.

"No, but I hear they act like they have something stuck up their butt!" I laughed.

"Honey, if you ever meet one, please run. Heaven's sake, don't speak to him. He's liable to throw the gates of hell open and push you through," Nestor warned. I turned to see if he was joking, but behind his smirk, I saw a twinge of fear. If he'd met an angel, I'd like to hear that story.

"I've met an angel. She's sitting next to you," Levi said ogling Kady. Kadence Rayburn was the preacher's daughter. They met at church a couple of months ago. They hit it off so well, I could hardly stand to stay with them in the trailer. If the trailer was rocking... I would sleep on Nestor's couch. He lived in a small apartment above the bar.

Kady was a healthy girl with curves in all the right places. Her brown doe eyes drew my bard's attentions from the moment he met her. For now, she made him happy. The day she stopped, I would end her.

"Aw," she cooed. She blew him a kiss, and he caught it. Young, stupid love.

I rolled my eyes. "Gag a maggot," I teased.

"Where's Dylan?" Kady asked.

"I am not Dylan's keeper," I replied.

"She knows exactly where he is at all times. He reports in regularly," Levi responded.

"At this very moment, I do not know where he is, Levi Rearden. How dare you call me a liar?" I said. "Honey, the tree is straight now. Leave it alone."

"Okay, cool. Now I can hang these lights," he said, dipping into the box of decorations that Nestor gave us to put up around the bar. I'd already hung green and red tinsel around the edges. It was tangled up when I took it out of the box. About an hour later, I had it sorted.

"I'll help," Kady said, leaving me alone at the bar. The Hot Tin Roof Bar was the only watering hole in Shady Grove, Alabama. My grandfather ran it. Nestor Gwinn was a kelpie.

A kelpie, an equine water fairy that lures passersby in order to trap them into their aquatic abode, was kind of fitting for the barkeep. However, he had no plans on drowning his patrons. It's hard to get repeat sales when the customer is deceased.

Levi Rearden was a changeling, the first bard born into the known world in over a hundred years. I was his patron, Grace Ann Bryant, Trailer Park Queen. Actually, my official title was Queen of the Exiles, but I lived in a double wide, proudly sported a large tattoo on my right arm, and liked my shorts very short. However, it was December, so I wore tight chocolate leggings with a burgundy tunic. Tall brown boots and a plaid scarf at my neck. Kady picked the outfit out. She said I looked cute.

Shady Grove's population was riddled with exiled fairies. Since I became their Queen a few months ago, the town had grown exponentially. Many exiled fairies got the word that a Queen had emerged to protect them. When I agreed to this role, I didn't realize the trouble I was getting myself into, but here I was.

I turned my back on the love birds. They made me sick with all their touchy-feely crap. Nestor shook his head at me. The bar was mostly empty. One patron sat at the end of the bar with beady eyes munching on the free peanuts. He had an empty bottle of cheap beer.

"May I have another cup?" I asked. Nestor made magical coffee. It not only warmed your body, but it soothed your soul. It seemed my soul needed a lot of soothing lately.

"Sure," he said refilling my cup. "So, where *is* Dylan?"

"He drove into Tuscaloosa to get some paperwork for this fool idea of becoming a private investigator," I said.

"Grace, the guy is not a sheriff anymore. Why is it a fool idea?" Nestor asked.

"Because, what's he gonna do? Stake out cow pastures for tippers?" I asked.

Nestor laughed. "I'm sure he will find plenty of cases with the influx of fairies we've had lately," he replied. He was right. Things were getting hectic around here.

"I suppose," I grumbled. Levi had passed his bah humbug to me.

"You really don't want him to do it? What's he supposed to do, Grace? Follow you around everywhere?" Nestor said.

"No, I'm still mad at him," I replied.

"You've got to get over that," he chided. I wasn't really mad at Dylan Riggs who had managed to get himself shot trying to save me. He died actually, but unbeknownst to me, he was a phoenix rising from the ashes. He lied to me about a lot of things before and after he died. His death rocked me in a way I never imagined possible. We had a long friendship, a torrid one-night stand, and several months of bickering. Then he died, forcing me to realize how important was to me. I just wasn't ready, after hundreds of years to commit to someone.

As a fairy, my hormones and inclination for sexual connection erupt far more than the normal human. It made it hard for me to tell the difference between lust and love. However, when Dylan died, it ripped me to pieces. When he returned, I was madder than hell. We still spent time together, but we played a game where he would ask for a reprieve of my anger in small increments of time.

"I'm afraid that if he gets involved with police work that he might die again," I admitted quietly to Nestor. Long before I realized Nestor was my grandfather, he was my bartender. He listened to my problems, supplied my alcohol, and gave sound advice. I hadn't drunk very much since Dylan returned. Nestor's supernatural coffee was enough to soothe my apprehensions.

"Fortunately for him he can rise from the dead," Nestor pointed out.

"Yes, but is there a limit on that kind of thing? Is there a way to kill him where he won't come back?" I shuddered at my own statement. Sitting my cup down, I wrung my hands trying to calm the shaking. The mere thought of it terrified me.

Nestor laid a warm hand over mine and stared at me. "Grace, we only get one life. Granted most of us have lived longer than we ever imagined, but you have to make the most of the time you have. Don't let your fear of losing him keep you apart. Most of this town knows exactly how you feel about each other, even if you won't admit it."

"Hmph," I grunted and turned back to the young couple hanging lights. "Looks good, guys!"

The lights added a twinkle to the normally darkened bar. Nestor's bar wasn't exactly a dive, but it certainly wasn't like the fancy ones I'd seen in photographs. I loved magazines, especially tabloids. I loved spending time at the bar. Finally, I was able to return after I spent so much time away from it after Dylan and I hooked up the first time.

As if on cue, the bar door swung open, and Mr. Sandy Hair came in from the cold. His brilliant blue eyes flashed when they met my eyes. When his smile stretched across his face, I was undone. He never looked at Levi or Kady when they greeted him. Striding forward to the bar next to me, he tapped on it lightly as Nestor poured him a warm cup of coffee. He dumped two spoons of sugar into it and took a sip.

"It's cold enough to freeze the tits off a frog," he exclaimed. Levi and Kady laughed.

"Frogs don't have tits," I said, not looking at him.

"I beg your pardon, my Queen," he said, insisting on referring to me in that infernal way. "But I do remember a biology class long, long ago where we dissected a frog, and it most certainly had tits."

"You were never in a biology class," I proclaimed, finally looking up at him.

Leaning over to whisper in my ear, he said, "Five seconds."

"You can't do anything meaningful in five seconds," I replied.

"Please," he begged. I melted.

"Five seconds," I said, starting to count silently in my head. He wrapped his arm around my waist, and I could feel the radiating warmth of his body.

"Beautiful Grace," he muttered. Pressing his lips to my cheek, he pulled away the moment I reached five in my head.

Chills ran down my spine, and I gulped. Five seconds was plenty to make the fairy whore inside of me turn cartwheels.

"Meaningful?" he asked.

"I suppose," I replied suppressing the desire to make out with him in front of everyone. He sat down on the stool next to me and watched Levi hanging lights around the room.

"The tree looks good," he said.

"Yes, once Levi finally got it straight. But I agree that it does look mighty fine," I declared. Levi grinned at my admission that he'd done a good job. Kady rubbed his shoulder drawing his attention away from Dylan and me.

"You get your paperwork done?" I asked.

"I just picked it up. I'll work on completing it after the holidays," he said.

The bar door swung open again, and the new sheriff, Troy Maynard walked in, bringing a wave of cold with him.

"Lord have mercy. Shut that door, Troy. You are letting the heat out," I proclaimed.

"Grace! I've been looking for you," he said exasperated. I looked down at my phone, but I hadn't missed a call. He noticed and continued, "I didn't call. I figured you'd be here. Oh, hey Dylan."

"Troy," Dylan acknowledged him. Dylan used to be the sheriff until his involvement with me got him suspended, and like the romantic moron that he was, he quit his job for me. I adored him for it, but of course, I refused to admit it. Either way, he knew. I hoped.

"I need you to come down to holding. We've got a guy down there whom we dragged out of Deacon Giles' field. He's demanding to see the Queen, and raising hell. Will you please come talk to him?" he begged.

"She can't just show up for every misguided fairy," Dylan protested. Laying my hand over his, I squeezed.

"What was he doing in the field?" I asked.

"Terrorizing the livestock," Troy replied.

"You mean he was, um, doing *it* with them?" I asked. My mind wallowed in the gutter. Fairy.

"No! Not that. He was chasing the sheep, making the goats faint and tipping the cows," he sighed.

"Sounds rather fun to me," I giggled as Dylan poked me in the side. "Come on, let's go talk to a fool."

Leaving Levi and Kady to finish decorating, Dylan drove me down to the sheriff's department. "I'm sorry if I interfered," he said.

"You're right, I've gotten myself into one hell of a mess, but I'm good at that, aren't I?" I asked trying to prevent him from feeling guilty for caring about me.

"You most certainly are, but this queen thing has gotten out of hand. Every time you turn around some forlorn fairy is begging for your protection," he said. "You can't possibly protect them all."

"Just accepting who I am provides a measure of protection. I've virtually claimed the exotic town of Shady Grove as my kingdom, and my palace is a double wide," I smirked.

"You make light of it, but I know you got more than you bargained for when you accepted all of this. I'm sorry if I pushed you into it," he said.

"I did get more than I anticipated, but Dylan, I don't blame you, so stop being so dammed forlorn. It's the holidays. Let's celebrate and have fun," I suggested.

He squeezed my hand as we pulled into the lot outside the sheriff's department. "As you wish, my Queen."

"Quit fucking calling me that," I protested. He finally laughed.

"Vulgar mouth," he said turning to me.

"One minute," I offered as he stared at me.

"I didn't ask for a minute," he protested.

"I read your mind," I smiled.

"You did not," he replied.

"Fine. My bad," I said grabbing the door handle.

"Um, no," he said pulling me to him and covering my mouth with his. I lost count around twenty-two. But approximately a minute later, he rested his forehead on mine, "Do you know how hard it is to count while doing that?"

"Actually, it's easy. You were two seconds short," I replied.

"Damn you, Grace," he grumbled, getting out of the car. I climbed out before he could open the door for me, watching him scowl. He took my hand as we entered his former place of employment.

❄

We walked past receiving through a set of double swinging doors to the entrance to the holding cells. It wasn't so long ago that I inhabited one of the cells after being accused of murder. Thankfully, those charges were dropped.

Bellows assaulted our ears as we entered the cell room. "I'm not talking to nobody, but the queen. You bring her here to me. I demand it. It's my right," he screamed, filling the room with his screeching.

Stopping in my tracks, Dylan almost ran over me, but he froze as we both laid eyes on the bellower. He stood around five and half foot tall with gangly arms and bulging eyes. His hands hung too long past his waist. His long boney fingers twitched as he protested. However, beyond this strange appearance, he teetered on a long, wooden peg leg.

"You've got to be fucking kidding me," I mumbled. Dylan suppressed a laugh behind me as I elbowed him. "Enough of that racket. I'm here. What the hell do you want?"

He leveled his beady eyes on me and grumped, "You ain't no queen. You look like trailer trash."

Dylan snorted behind me, and I whipped around on him. He held his hands up in surrender as my eyes flashed turquoise. Shaking my head to release the anger, I looked at him again, conveying my contrition the best I could without speaking. "It's okay. Do your thing," he urged. He knew tapping into the fairy queen made me jumpy.

Turning back to the old man who continued to demand to see the queen, I pulled power stored in my tattoo, and my glamour dropped revealing the Ice Queen within me. "Silence!" I demanded. I'll admit that since I'd embraced my new calling, I felt like I could control Gloriana, my true fairy name. I was the daughter of the King of the Unseelie Fairies in the Otherworld, Oberon. My mother, one of his many concubines, was the first to ever provide him with a female heir. I'd subsequently gotten into enough trouble to get banished from his realm, and we had only recently reconnected. He seemed to have finally accepted my decision to live amongst humans, but only once I decided to lead the other exiles here.

My sparkling silver gown stretched to the floor shimmering under the cool fluorescent glow of the holding cell. The room turned colder as frost formed on the bars between the gangly fairy and myself.

"My Queen," he said, trying to bow, but his peg leg slid on the concrete. He found himself before me on his knees.

Suppressing an immature laugh, I asked, "Why have you called me here?"

"Forgive me, but these human lawmen do not understand our ways. I hoped you would intercede for me in allowing me to leave this jail. I meant no harm to the creatures. I love animals. See," he said screwing his peg leg off to show me intricate carvings of various animals all around it. "I'm working on this new one here. It's a wild hog, a razorback." He beamed proudly at his craftsmanship, but once his eyes turned to my cold, blank stare, he gulped.

I stood transfixed by the utter ridiculousness of the situation. I put my hand up politely refusing to hold his wooden leg. "Why were you torturing Mr. Giles' livestock?" I asked, standing over him.

"It's just what I do. How I have fun," he said.

"You will not do this in my city. Do you understand? I cannot intercede if you are a menace!" I replied with force.

He cowered before me. "Yes, my Queen, please forgive me."

"The fairies in this town live by the rule of law. I see to it that they do. In turn, I protect them. However, if they cross the line, they pray that Sheriff Maynard catches them before I do," I informed him.

"Yes, ma'am, I understand," he said, leaning forward and kissing my shoe.

"What's your name?" I asked.

"Lamar," he replied.

"Well, Lamar, you will spend the night here. If you simmer down, Sheriff Maynard will let you leave tomorrow. However, you must promise me that you will not torture any more livestock." I said.

"I promise," he muttered, sounding defeated.

"Cow tipping?" I questioned.

A large grin passed over his face. "Yep, with my peg leg. I just tap them with it, and kaboom, they flop over," he giggled. His laugh sounded like a donkey, and he slapped his knee for good measure. "Only that last time, the cow fell the wrong way, and I got caught."

"The cow fell *on* you?" I asked.

"Yep, he pinned me good. I was hollering for help, but the *good* farmer left me there while the lawmen were called," he grumped.

"Serves you right," I said with a smile. "Cow tipping is a heinous crime."

"Thank you, my Queen," he replied.

I turned swiftly before I died laughing in front of him. Dylan continued to smirk behind me. My glamour popped back into place as we passed through the doors. Hurrying to the front door, I let loose as my laugh echoed through the parking lot. Dylan joined me as tears of humor formed in the corners of his eyes. "You've got to be kidding me," he said.

"With my peg leg," I replied poking at him with my finger. We continued to laugh when Troy stepped out of the building.

"Good grief," he exclaimed. "Thank you, Grace. He would not shut up. It's been like that for hours. The guys were about to lose their minds."

I waved my hand at him, "No problem, Wolf." Troy Maynard was a werewolf. One of the few who weren't fairies in this town.

"Y'all have a good night," he said, turning back to the warmth of the station.

"Will you take me home, Dylan?" I asked, gathering my senses.

"It will be my pleasure," he replied.

"You aren't staying," I added.

"I know. You are still mad at me," he said.

"But I'll give you an hour," I smiled.

"I can do a lot of things in an hour," his face brightened. "Come on, let's go!" He eagerly pulled me to his car, practically shoving me in the passenger seat. My laughter returned as he tore out of the parking lot, heading for my double wide.

WAKING UP TO THE SMELL OF COFFEE BREWING HAS TO BE THE MOST glorious way to wake up. However, alone in a cold bed isn't so fun. I jumped up, starting the warm water in the shower when I heard Dylan's voice in the living room.

I threw open the door and stared at him. "Well, good morning, Sunshine," he quipped.

"Your hour was up a long time ago!" I protested.

"Yes, it was. I went home, slept and returned this morning. Levi invited me in for coffee," he explained, kicking Levi in the shin.

"Ow, um, yeah, coffee," Levi said, flicking channels on the television. He took a sip of his coffee, eyeballing me over the rim of the cup. Both of them waited with bated breath for my reaction.

I huffed, turned on my heels, slamming the bedroom door. Listening intently, I heard them both suppressing laughs. The bastards.

My shower didn't last as long as I had wished because I heard a commotion in the other room. Jumping back out of the shower, I grabbed a robe and wrapped my hair in a towel. As I entered the room, I found Levi clutching a crying Winnie in his arms.

"What's wrong?" I exclaimed, rushing to her. Levi eyed my robe as it slipped open, and I growled at him.

"There is a man in the refrigerator," she cried into Levi's shoulder.

"What!" I said.

"Dylan went over there," he nodded toward the door.

I went to the door and stared at the trailer across the street. I liked Bethany Jones, but she had issues. I loved her child, Wynonna, and did whatever I could for the angel. However, Winnie recently became more attached to Uncle Levi more than Aunt Grace, which was a blow to my ego.

Opening the door, I started out into the cold in a robe, wet hair and bare feet. Mid-December in Alabama isn't like in Michigan or Norway. It can actually be very mild, but lately we had frigid temps. Even with the sun rising to its apex, there was a thick layer of frost on the ground.

"You are going to get sick, Grace! Your hair is wet," Levi shouted at me through the screen door.

"I'm the fucking Ice Queen, Levi!" I shouted back at him, but admonished myself for using the 'f' word in front of Winnie. Ice Queen or not, it was freezing. I hurried across the street hearing muffled noises from the trailer. A scream tore through the air, and I sprinted with the bottom of my robe flinging around my legs. Hopefully, the rest of the park was asleep otherwise they probably got a good view.

I stormed into the trailer, finding Dylan on the floor wrestling with a strange looking man. A whole gallon of milk poured onto the linoleum floor as Bethany cowered in the corner. Dylan locked arms with him and forced him to the floor with his knee in the man's back. The man howled in pain.

"Get down, mother fucker," Dylan yelled. "Vulgar mouth," I said as he grimaced at me.

"My Queen," the man said, ceasing to struggle and putting his face to the floor.

"Oh, hell," I said. Staring at the man, I realized that his features favored the idiot from the jail last night. His arms were long and gangly. Beady black eyes stared at the floor as he paid reverence to me. I shot a look at Bethany who was actually one of the few complete humans in the town. "Get him out of here, Dylan."

"Yes, ma'am," he said, hauling the fairy man up and dragging him out of the trailer.

"You okay?" I asked Bethany. She nodded silently. "Winnie is with Levi. I don't suspect she will want to come back for a few hours. We will take the intruder down to the jail, Okay?"

She nodded again as I left the trailer with no other explanation. She looked half out of her mind. I wasn't sure if it was from the intruder or if she'd had a long drug trip overnight.

As I crossed the road, Dylan threw the idiot into the back of my truck and tied his hands with some rope. "Get some clothes on before you get sick, Grace," he told me.

"Just a minute," I said. "Who the hell are you?"

"Your humble servant," he said, bowing his head.

"Your humble ass is going to sit in the back of my truck until I come back. Got it?" I said.

"Yes, my Queen," he responded.

Dylan gritted his teeth, staring at me in my robe. "Okay! Okay!" I said flinging my hands up in frustration.

Quickly, I threw on some jeans and a sweater. Adding warm socks and boots to my ensemble, I watched as Levi clicked the television over to cartoons as Winnie sobbed in his arms.

"You okay, Winnie?" I asked her, smoothing her brown hair down with my hand. She still wore a pair of worn princess pajamas and sparkly purple house shoes.

"Yes, Uncle Levi will protect me," she whimpered.

"Yes, he will. Aunt Grace and Mr. Dylan are going to take the bad man down to the jail," I said.

"Okay," she muttered.

"Where's Kady?" I asked.

"She had to go home last night to prepare for something for church," he replied. "I'll stay here with Winnie. We are going to watch cartoons and color."

"Feed her," I said. He nodded in response.

Grabbing Dylan's leather jacket off the back of the couch, I walked through the screen door. Dylan waited for me in the yard. He took the soft leather jacket and shrugged it on. I had found the jacket in my closet after his death. It was a huge comfort to me. It smelled like Dylan. Leather, peppermint and musk. He watched me staring at the jacket.

"You want it? You know I'll give it to you," he said softly.

"No, silly. Just memories," I said. He grimaced and ran his fingers down my cheek. "I'll deduct those two seconds from you next request."

That made him smile. "In that case," he said, stepping closer to me.

"No, let's get this jerk wad down to the sheriff," I pushed him away. Turning to the milk thief, I asked, "So, what's your name?"

His eyes rose to mine, and he said, "My beautiful Queen, my name is Phil, and I will forever be your servant. You are the sun on a beautiful morning, the air on a crisp day…"

"Yeah, yeah. Clam it up," I said, shutting him down. "Hope you don't mind the cold, but you aren't getting in the cab of my truck."

"I will be satisfied to just be in your vehicle, my Queen," he continued.

Dylan chuckled behind me. "Hush your mouth, Dylan," I said trying not to laugh.

We climbed in the truck, and I let Dylan drive. He was still laughing.

"What the hell is going on in this town?" I asked.

"I don't know, but it's hilarious," he continued.

"Drive, Mr. Riggs," I said.

"You need a nickname for me," he said, backing the truck out of the drive.

"Like what?"

"I'd prefer something manly," he replied.

"Like Pumpkin?" I asked.

"No, not Pumpkin. That's what a man calls a girl," he said.

"Well, what do you want me to call you?" I asked.

"I don't know. You are supposed to pick it out," he proclaimed.

"How about, Slave?" I asked.

"Keep dreaming," he said.

"I dream of you quite often," I replied.

"Gunngh," he swallowed his words. Without looking at me, I could tell his blue eyes were glittering. "Ahem! Oh, really? I hadn't realized."

He made me laugh. "Yeah, sure. 101 ways to torture Dylan Riggs."

"Aw, Grace. Last night *was* torture," he said.

"What? It's not my fault that you got lost in the kissing and time ran out. You should use your time more wisely," I said. We hadn't been together since that first night a long, long time ago. Three whole months. I desperately wanted him, but for some reason, I kept delaying the inevitable. He certainly had the opportunity last night, but perhaps, I wasn't the only one timid about renewing our sexual contact.

"If you would just quit playing games and admit that you forgive me, we would both be better off," he protested.

"Perhaps," I said.

"Perhaps? Is that all you can say?" Suddenly we weren't flirting anymore. As his frustration grew, I shrank back into my guarded cocoon. I gritted my teeth, searching for the right words to say, but we had reached our destination. Sitting at the wheel, he waited for me to respond. He slapped it hard with the palm of his hand and climbed out grumbling. As I slid out of my side of the truck, I felt like a piece of crap.

He untied the weird looking fellow and dragged him toward the door of the jail. A couple of deputies standing in the parking lot recognized Dylan.

"Hey, Riggs, you need some help?" one of them called out.

"No, I've got it," he responded hauling the guy to the door. "I need my head examined."

The strange man started to buck away from Dylan. "No, my Queen, please don't execute me. These men execute wrong doers."

"I execute wrong doers," I spouted at him with more frustration with Dylan than for this crazed fool. "What were you doing in that house?"

"Taking milk," he responded. "I love milk."

I looked at Dylan, and he shrugged.

"You are going inside to think about what you did wrong. You can't just go into people's houses and steal milk!" I said.

He hung his head and said, "Yes, my Queen. But I got in trouble once before taking mother's milk, so I switched to whole cow's milk."

"Mother's milk?" I asked.

"Yes, right from the source," he cooed.

"Holy hell," I choked out.

Dylan escorted him into receiving and explained the situation to the desk officer. She was a plump woman with a name tag that said, C. Dawson. "Morning, Carol," Dylan said.

"What did you drag in here, Dylan Riggs?" she exclaimed, but instead of looking at the man, she flicked her eyes to me. Bitch.

Licking her lips, she fluttered her eyelids at him. The possessive fairy inside me reared her nasty head snarling at Carol Dawson.

I looked at her through my royal fairy sight to determine if she was human or fairy. She glowed green around the edges, so I knew she was a fairy. I was still trying to tell the difference between different types of fairies, but clearly, she belonged to the woodland realm. However, I only glanced at her as my eyes were drawn to the pulsing heat of fire that rolled over Dylan's form. It was warm and inviting.

I leaned over the counter toward Carol who rolled back in her chair. "Mine," I growled. She nodded her head as fear filled her eyes. Generally, I made idle threats, but the one I laid on Carol with a single word came from that dark place inside of me.

"Grace?" Dylan said, as an officer took Phil from him, escorting the awkward man to the holding cells.

I shook off the anger and stared back at him. "Sorry. Zoned out," I said.

"You okay?" he asked suddenly concerned. His frustration washed away like it never happened.

"Yeah, just weird things happening. That's all," I explained.

Then we heard a commotion in the holding cells. Dylan rushed to the door. As I followed him closely, the two weird men embraced each other inside the cell.

"Brother!" Lamar said to Phil.

"Brother!" Phil said, patting his brother on the back.

"What the fuck?" I muttered.

"Mouth," Dylan said.

"Bite me," I said.

"How long do I have to do that?" he asked. I blushed, turning away from him.

As I walked over to the cell, the officer stood stunned at the two idiots hugging and patting each other. "You are brothers?"

"Oh, my Queen! It's so good to see you this morning," Lamar said, without me turning into Gloriana.

"Good morning to you, as well. Did you behave last night? Is the sheriff going to let you leave this morning?" I asked.

"No, I've decided to stay with my brother, my Queen. I feel for certain that if you let me out, I would tip more cows," he explained, scratching his peg leg.

I cocked my head sideways watching him scratch it. Dylan snorted right behind me, and I jumped. "Sorry," he muttered through laughs.

"This town has gone insane," I replied.

"It's always been crazy. You are just now noticing," he replied.

"Apparently," I said taking his hand leaving the weird-o

brothers behind. As we walked out the door, I cut my eyes to Carol Dawson who stared at us muttering something under her breath.

When we pulled into the drive at the trailer, Dylan sat in the truck and didn't move. I sighed, knowing he wanted to talk about us.

"Never mind," he said getting out of the truck.

"Wait, Dylan!" I protested. "Wait, please, say what you were going to say."

"It's cold out here, and you've already been traipsing around in bare feet. You need to get inside," he instructed.

"No, come on, I can't get sick," I replied.

"Inside!" he demanded, pointing toward the door.

Entering the room, Levi was seated at the table coloring with Winnie. His face flashed with concern when he saw me. I shook my head at him, heading toward my room. "You eat, Winnie?" I asked passing her.

"Yes, ma'am. Uncle Levi made me toast and let me put strawberry jam on it," she said.

"Yummy," I replied.

"It was delish," she replied.

Looking back at Dylan standing at the door, I motioned to my room. He shook his head. "No, I'm going home."

"Please don't," I begged.

"Call you later," he said, heading back out in the cold.

"What happened?" Levi asked.

Closing my eyes, I wondered if I should chase him. I heard his car rumble to life, and I headed toward the door. Slinging the door open, I paced out on to the wooden deck. He looked up from the dash and pointed back at the trailer. I could see him mouthing the words, "Get back inside!"

"No!" I said with my hands on my hips.

He grimaced, pulled out, and sped away.

For the rest of the day I flipped from cussing the day I met Dylan Riggs to being on the verge of tears, thinking he wouldn't come back. I checked my phone every 5 minutes, working myself into a tizzy. For years I'd watched other women do the same thing about a certain man and scoffed at their immaturity, but here I was doing the same damn thing.

Levi played with Winnie most of the day, but before bed, she insisted that she go home. She said her mommy needed her. I winced. A six-year-old child taking care of her mother. The thought just added to my already terrible day.

"You know he will come back," Levi said.

"One day he won't. He will give up on me," I replied.

"No, you just need to get over whatever it is holding you back," Levi said.

"Thank you, love guru," I snarled.

"Truth hurts," he said as he went into his bedroom shutting the door.

I stood at the kitchen sink, looking down the road toward town. After an hour, I stopped looking for him and went to bed.

DECEMBER 14TH

AROUND 1 A.M. MY PHONE BUZZED TO LIFE. REACHING OVER IN THE darkness, I plucked it from the nightstand. Mr. Riggs had finally decided to talk to me.

"Are you awake?" the text said.

"Yes," I responded. Within just a moment, the phone rang. I answered it quickly, "Hello?"

"I'm sorry," he immediately said. "I'm sorry for everything. I'd do it differently now, Grace. Please, I just…" His voice cut off.

"I'm just afraid, Dylan," I admitted.

"Open the door," he said.

"What?" I replied.

"I'm at the front door, and I didn't want to knock," he said. I jumped out of bed and ran to the front door. When I let him in, the cold air from outside rushed in. He shut the door behind him, then wrapped me in his arms. The leather jacket was cool, but his hands were warm. Tossing the jacket on the back of the couch, he guided me back to the bedroom, shutting the door behind us.

Leaning against it, he stared at me. "Afraid of what?" he asked.

"Losing you again," I replied truthfully. "You can die, obviously. But is there a limit? Can you be extinguished?"

"Interesting choice of words," he replied. "There is no limit, but yes, just like you, I can cease to be. However, it would take the power of a royal fairy to do it or something as strong."

"Oh," I said. "I would never."

"I know," he said, leaning his forehead to mine. "I need to hear you say it."

"Say what? What time is it?" I asked.

"Grace, I do not want to play this game," he said sternly.

Pulling out my phone, I said, "It's 1:37 am. You have six hours."

"I want you to say you forgive me. I want forever," he replied.

Stepping away from him, my heart pounded in my chest. It wasn't *the* three words, but it was pretty darn close. "You admit that this whole queen thing a mess. I don't want you dragged down by it," I made up an excuse.

"I do not care, Grace. You stubborn woman!" he exhaled. "You marched into a forest to save a little girl, taking on an Aswang and a werewolf. You stood up to your father, the king of the Wild Fae. How in the world are you afraid of me?"

"I'm not afraid of you," I muttered.

"Then what are you afraid of?" he begged.

"Us," I sighed.

"I'm not," he replied, stepping back towards me. "Forever means I'll wait that long if I have to."

"Aw, why do you have to be like that?" I groaned.

"Because, sometimes dealing with stubborn women, the best thing you can do is make her feel bad," he replied frankly.

"I should slap you," I said. He turned around and offered his ass. "Oh, stop. I already knew you were an ass."

He plopped down on the bed, patting the mattress beside him. "Take your shoes off," I demanded.

"Yes, ma'am" he replied. As he finished, I laid down next to him snuggling up to his warmth. I'd never been sick before, but I had a definite chill from my excursion in the bathrobe. "Grace, you feel warm to me."

He placed his hand on my forehead. "I think you have a temperature," he said.

"No, I can't get sick," I replied.

"No, you've never been sick. Two different things, my dear," he said. "Just lay here and rest. I'll take care of you."

"You want me to be sick," I replied.

"Never," he said as I drifted off to sleep next to the warm body of a phoenix.

Startled, I jumped up in the bed. My head swam around in the darkness of the room as sweat poured down my face.

"Grace, what's wrong?"

"I think I'm sick," I replied.

"I told you," he said, running his hand up my back under my shirt. His normally warm hands felt cool to me as I shivered to his touch. "Damn, you are burning up."

Reaching over to grab his cell phone, he dialed, "Sorry to bother you this early, but she's sick." My upright body swayed as I tried to concentrate on his conversation. Gently, he pushed back me down flat on the bed. "No, nothing like that, but she's running a fever."

Then I heard Nestor's voice clearly, "Take her to the med center to see Dr. Mistborne. She's a fairy doc. If anyone can figure it out, it will be her. I'll meet you down there."

"Alright, but you stay. I'll call you once we speak to the doc. I'm taking her now," Dylan said hanging up the phone. As he leaned over the bed to put on his shoes, I drifted in and out.

"Darlin', we can go in the morning," I sputtered.

"No, we are going now," he said as he turned to lift me off the bed. Weakness caused my arms to loll with no tension. He carried me effortlessly to the living room. "Levi!"

"What's going on?" Levi asked, emerging from his room scratching his head.

"Grace is sick. Do you have the truck keys?" Dylan asked.

Levi ducked back into his room and returned with the keys. "I'm going too," he said grabbing his sweats.

"Grab a blanket," Dylan ordered, hauling me out the front door into the cold.

"I'm scared," I muttered.

"It's okay. Just a cold or something," he replied, trying to convince both of us.

Dylan climbed in the passenger seat as Levi started the truck. The once staunch sheriff actually rode without his seatbelt on so that he could keep his arms around me. The streets of Shady Grove were dark as we passed through the main part of town. The lighted decorations covered in tinsel hung from the main power poles as we passed. Candy canes, angels and snowflakes glittered in the darkness.

Pulling into the med center, Levi lead the way as Dylan continued to carry me. My head rested close to his neck. Despite the sickness, my hormones started flip-flopping as I drank in his scent.

Levi gave all my information to the receptionist even though Jessica knew me from church.

Our church looked like your run of the mill southern Baptist church on the outside. But once you stepped inside, it became a glorious grove of towering oak and ash trees. The pastor was a druid. The fairies of the town met there every Sunday. It was a social gathering more than anything. In the last few weeks, Dylan and I had discussed starting a council to talk over fairy matters which seemed to grow on a weekly basis.

A nurse whom I did not know directed us to a small cubicle behind a white curtain. Dylan gently laid me on the bed. I felt like I'd been beaten with a stick. My head felt woozy again. The nurse asked a hundred questions about my illness and its onset. Dylan answered most of them. Then she blurted out, "Mr. Riggs, are you Miss Bryant's next of kin?"

"Um, no," he said.

"Fiancé?" she asked.

"No, ma'am," he replied. She tapped her pencil on her teeth.

"I'm afraid you are going to have to wait in the waiting room like everyone else. Next of kin only back here," she explained.

"No," I muttered. "I want him to stay."

"I'm sorry, Miss Bryant. It's policy," she said.

Gathering what little strength I had left, I raised up and said, "Fuck your policy. He's not leaving me."

"Grace, honey, lay back. It's okay. I'll be right down the hall with Levi," he tried to calm me.

"No, don't go," I whimpered. "Call Remy. He will draw up the paperwork to fix this. I need you here."

His face twisted, because I knew he didn't want Remington Blake anywhere near me, but he was my lawyer now since Demetrius Lysander decided to be an ASS-wang. My father killed him for his treachery.

"Okay. Nothing will stop me from coming in this room if you need me," he said.

"I don't need you locked up with the creepy brothers," I replied. A hint of a smile brightened in his eyes, but did not reach his lips. However, he leaned over gently kissing me on my lips.

"You can take that one out of the next time, too," he said with his face so close to mine.

"That one is free," I replied. The smile finally found his lips.

"Out! Now!" the nurse exclaimed, reaching her patience plateau.

"It's okay," I assured him.

The door clicked behind him as the nurse scowled shoving a needle into my IV.

"Goodnight," she smirked. My eyes fluttered drifting off into a deep sleep.

A sharp clang rattled me awake. When my eyes opened, I stared at the top of a slightly balding head with liver spots. The man was bent down at the edge of my bed, but as he raised to full height, I realized he was no more than 4 foot tall. His familiar beady eyes widened to see that I was awake. Over his shoulder, a mesh bag was slung holding at least four metal bed pans.

"What the fuck!" I exclaimed, as he backed away from me.

"My Queen, forgive me. I didn't mean to wake you," he bowed his head to me.

"Dylan!" I screamed. Rushing footsteps pounded down the hallway toward my room.

"Please, forgive, I was just collecting the bed pans," he replied.

"Do you work here?" I asked.

"Um, no," he admitted.

"Dylan!" I screamed again as the door slammed open. Dylan's worried expression changed to pure blue flame as he grabbed the little man by his collar throwing him against the wall. Levi came in the door dodging the flying man. The mesh bag hit the floor, and the pounding sound of metal clattered around the room.

"Help! My Queen! He will kill me! Have mercy! Have mercy!" he started to screech.

I covered my ears and winced. Levi leaned over me, "Did he hurt you?"

"No, he was just right here beside the bed when I woke up!" I trembled.

"Who are you?" Dylan growled. I heard more footsteps approaching.

"My name is Eric! I'm just collecting bed pans!" he replied. Dylan shot a look at me.

"He doesn't work here!" I explained.

"What are you doing with bed pans, sick bastard?" he asked.

"Well, I collect them and melt them down for projects at my house. But with these I'm going to make a beautiful water fountain in front of our house for my wife. I think I can run a hose pipe up in it and make it flow out all over the front lawn. Bless her, we have ten children. I thought I'd do something nice for her. Please my Queen, I didn't mean to wake you," he explained even though Dylan still held him by the neck against the wall.

Two security guards appeared at the door. "What's going on?"

"This guy doesn't belong here. He's stealing bed pans," Dylan explained.

"Oh, thanks for nabbing him, Mr. Riggs," the older gentleman said. "We will call the sheriff to come pick him up."

"Eric, do you have a brother named Lamar?" I asked.

"Hey! I do! You know my peg leg brother?" he asked. "He's a menace."

"He's waiting on you at the jail," I said.

"Oh, he was cow tipping again, wasn't he?" Eric said oblivious to his own menace.

The guards cuffed Eric, and he smiled at me as they dragged him out of the door. "Nice to meet you my Queen! You smell like cantaloupes!"

As the door shut behind the little man, Dylan looked at me dumbfounded. "Cantaloupes?"

"Hell, if I know! That's from a man making a bed pan fountain for his wife!" I said.

Levi died laughing. "What's going on in this town?"

"We need to find out if there are any other brothers!" I pointed out.

"Good idea," Dylan said smiling as he pulled out his phone. He put his warm hand in mine and squeezed.

"Remy came by. He dropped off some papers for you to sign," Levi said. I looked up to Dylan who squeezed my hand again. "We left them in the waiting room. I'll go get them. Kady is here to check on you, too."

"Good grief. Tell her thanks, but to go back home now, I'm feeling much better. I want to go home," I said.

Dylan hung up the phone, "Troy doesn't have any records on them, and Jeremiah hasn't responded to his calls."

"Jeremiah is back down in Louisiana chasing that voodoo witch again," I said after Levi left the room.

"He's never going to catch her," he said. "I don't know what difference it makes now. She can't touch Levi while he's under your protection."

"I think Jeremiah is more concerned that one-day Levi might decide to go back," I admitted.

"He'd be a fool," Dylan said. "And I'll beat him within an inch of his life for doing something that stupid."

"Dylan!" I exclaimed. "He's under my protection. If you hurt him, I'd hate to have to…"

"Do what? What are you going to do?" he teased.

"Something," I said.

"You already owe me ten hexes," he said.

"Eleven," I replied as he sat on the edge of the bed.

"My bad, I lost count. Empty promises are hard to remember," he continued to tease. "Do you really feel better?"

"Yes, I do," I said. "It was a blip, and now I want to go home. Please find Dr. Mistborne."

"Okay, sign those papers!" he said heading toward the door.

"I will," I replied.

Levi brought the papers after a few minutes, and his lips looked red and swollen.

"Y'all make out in the waiting room?" I asked.

"Grace," he growled at me.

"Your lips already told me," I laughed as I pushed myself up in the bed. The room spun around me for a minute. Levi rushed to my side dropping the papers on the floor. He steadied me by grabbing my arms just below my shoulders. "I'm fine. Just been lying down too long." I felt the strength in his hands as he gripped me. It was gentle, but firm. He hadn't touched me since Kady came into his life. We'd never had anything past a flirtation, because he knew my heart belonged to someone else.

Releasing my arm, he flexed his hand. "What was that?" he asked looking at his hand.

"What do you mean?"

"That tingle!" he said.

"Levi, you know that fairies feel differently from mortals. You've just forgotten, because you are engrossed with Kady," I said.

"You don't have to remind me that she won't live as long as me," he said, bitterly picking up the papers from the floor.

"I didn't mean it like that, Levi," I said apologetically.

"Whatever," he said slapping the folder down on my lap with a pen. "Glad you are better. I'll catch you later." His deep blue eyes brooded.

From the moment, I had met Levi Rearden he impressed me with his deep brooding skills. He was a bag of emotions and hormones. I loved him to death, but sometimes I wanted to slap some sense into him.

I only spoke to him once about Kady being a mortal. She was the daughter of the preacher who actually was a Druid priest. Just normal human beings. No supernatural elements. He was young and in love, again. At least this time, it wasn't a voodoo priestess.

I looked over the document, signing it making Dylan my power of attorney. I never imagined I'd need such a thing, but I supposed that now I did.

"Hey, you signed it," Dylan said. I hadn't heard him enter the room.

"Yes," I simply replied.

He kissed my forehead. "Thank you," he said. "I can't believe you did it without a protest."

"I don't protest everything!" I replied.

"Yes, you do," he accused.

"Take me home!" I begged.

"The doctor is on the way," he replied wrapping me up in his warm arms. I felt tingles when Levi touched me, but every time Dylan touched me it set my body on fire.

The doctor released me, and we went to my trailer together. Dylan settled me in the recliner waiting on my every need. I fell asleep in the recliner, but sometime later he carried me to bed curling his warm body around me.

DECEMBER 15TH

I PUSHED THE CART DOWN THE AISLE AT THE FOOD MART, gathering items to make for the Yule celebration the town was having on the Winter Solstice which was technically after the traditional Yule. The town regulars were used to Christmas celebrations, so we meshed them together in the interest of diversity. Levi followed behind me making suggestions. He'd looked up a traditional Yule celebration online and considered himself an expert now.

"I need to walk back over to the produce section," he said setting a bottle of cloves into the basket. "I forgot the oranges."

"Okay," I replied.

"You sure you are alright?" he asked.

"I'm fine. Go get your peaches," I said.

"Oranges!" he exclaimed. "You are a fairy. You should know about Yule!"

"I don't remember the celebrations at home, and everyone here does Christmas," I replied.

"I'll be back in a minute," he said running down the aisle.

He had taken Kady home the night before while I was still at the hospital. She wasn't spending the night like she used to when they first met. I hoped for his sake that they weren't fighting. I would hate to see his heart broken again.

When I rounded the corner on the aisle with pasta and other

dried goods, half-way down the aisle there was a display with various kitchen utensils. An extremely thin man stood in front of it, and he hitched hips to the side awkwardly. He caught me staring at him, so I looked away toward the pastas. As I slowly pushed the cart down the aisle, he moved toward the display as I got closer to him.

Levi came around the corner with a bag of oranges and stopped dead in his tracks looking at the man. I glanced toward the man, but he shuffled away making a tinkling sound. When I looked at Levi, he approached me quickly dropping the oranges in the cart, then passed me heading for the man.

Slinging him around by the shoulder, the awkward man dropped several items on the floor and they clattered around his feet.

"Levi, what are you doing?" I asked walking away from the cart to him.

Putting his hand in the air to stop me, he said, "Stop, Grace! Stay there."

I stopped and looked at the items on the floor. Five shining metal ladles laid on the floor at his feet. Taking a second look at the man, I realized he had something stuck in his pants.

"Thief! What are you doing?" Levi asked.

"Um, please don't hurt me," the man cried.

Mable Sanders, the cashier at the Food Mart and my favorite gossip, came around the corner to see what the commotion was. "What's going on, Levi?" She knew Levi from the times we'd visited Nestor Gwinn, my grandfather, at his newly built Hot Tin Roof Bar. She was dating my grandfather which in itself was weird.

"He's stealing spoons!" Levi said.

"Ladles," I corrected.

"What on earth?" Mable said.

The man stood switching his gaze to each of us. His eyes locked on me, and I knew what was coming.

"Oh hell," I muttered.

He dropped to his knees, "My Queen, forgive me. I was just getting a Christmas present for my wife!"

"I hate this fucking job," I muttered. "Levi, go get Dylan."

"I'm not leaving you here with him," he said holding the man by the collar.

"I'll go get him, Grace. Where is he?" Mable asked.

"Drinking coffee with Nestor," I replied.

"Okay, I'll call over there," she said heading back to the front counter.

"What's your name?" I asked the man.

"Cory," he replied.

"You got brothers?" I asked.

"Yes! I do. I can't wait for Christmas. We will all be together, and our mother will be in town," he beamed.

"Why are you stealing ladles for your wife?" I asked.

"Well, my Queen, every night when we get in bed, my wife says she wants a spoon. So, I decided to get her a bunch of big ass spoons. These are great, but I can't afford them," he said.

"Not a spoon, you idiot," Levi exclaimed.

"Levi!" I scolded him, and he rolled his eyes.

"Cory, your wife wants to cuddle," I explained.

"No ma'am, she said spoon."

I rubbed my forehead and felt dizzy for a moment. I didn't know whether to laugh or cry when Dylan came running from the front of the store.

"What the hell?" Dylan said, stopping to look at the ladles on the floor.

"His wife wanted to spoon," I explained.

Dylan's forehead wrinkled, then he looked at Levi who started laughing. He looked at the ladles, then up at me. I shrugged. "Buy the spoons!" Dylan yelled at him.

"I'm broke," he said jerking away from the laughing Levi. He stood and sprinted down the aisle. "I'm coming home with your spoons, baby!"

"Hey, you! Come back here," Levi yelled.

He and Dylan took off after the man who waved two ladles wildly as he ran out the automated front doors. Mable held her hand over her mouth in shock. I grabbed the cart and pulled it back to the ladles he left on the floor. Bending over to pick them up, the dizziness got stronger.

"Grace, you okay?" Mable asked.

"Yeah, just didn't sleep much," I replied.

"I'll get those. You go sit down in the front on the bench until Dylan gets back. You look pale. You were in the med center last night. You shouldn't be out here," she said steadying me.

"Maybe I should sit down," I said.

Mable braced me, but my knees weakened. I slid back down the floor holding myself upright with my hands on the floor.

"Grace, are you okay?" Mable asked. "I'm going to get Dylan."

I heard her feet pad away as the floor spun around my hands. Sweat poured down my face, dripping off my cheek to the tile below me. It would feel so good to lay down on the tile. It was cool, and I was tired. I decided to sleep.

When I woke up, Dylan had cradled me in his arms. We sat on the floor at the Food Mart. Mable stood over her shoulder talking to someone on a cell phone.

"What the hell are you doing?" Dylan asked as he brushed hair out of my face. The sweat made it cling to my forehead and cheeks.

"I wanted to sleep," I muttered.

"On the floor at the Food Mart?" he asked playfully, but I saw the fear in his eyes.

"Stop. I'm fine," I said.

"No, you aren't. We are going back to the Med Center," he said pushing himself off the floor with me in his arms. He was stronger than I thought.

"You are so strong," I said smiling at him.

"Maybe I like you better delirious," he smirked.

"Nah! You like it when I torture you," I said.

"Yeah, I do. But right now, we need to find out what's making you sick," he said.

"It's these ladle-stealing idiots," I said.

He tilted his head sideways as we walked toward the front door. Levi sat on the front bench in the store holding Cory down by his collar. "What's wrong?" he asked Dylan

"Relapse," Dylan said. "Stay with him. Troy will be here in a minute."

"But…" Levi protested.

"Levi!" Dylan let his frustration out on my bard.

"Don't talk to him like that," I scolded Dylan.

"Grace! You are sick. Shut your mouth!" Dylan fussed back at me.

"Put me down," I said pushing away from him. I dug the heel of my hand into his chest.

For a moment, I thought he was going to throw me on the floor. Instead, he tightened his grip on me and stared at me. "Grace, please stop," he pleaded.

"Well, since you said please," I replied as the effort to push his chest made my head swim again. I laid my head back on his shoulder and finished my nap.

WAKING UP IN A DARKENED ROOM WITH MONITORS BEEPING, I KNEW I was back in the med center. I didn't stir, but opened my eyes looking around the room. In the recliner across the room, Nestor Gwinn slept. Just over the end of the bed, I could see Levi sitting on the floor asleep. In a chair next to the bed, Dylan sat sleeping with his head on the edge of my bed. The curtains were drawn, but a vein of light peeked through declaring the sun had risen on a new day.

Slowly I lifted my hand, brushing it through Dylan's sandy hair. His blue eyes opened slowly, then he realized I was looking back at him and bolted up to touch my face. He rested his head on my forehead.

"Grace," he whispered. It was enough to awaken the other two men. Levi stood up from the floor stretching. Nestor leaned forward in the chair with worried eyes fixed on me.

"Why do you all look so bad?" I asked.

"It was a rough night," Dylan said.

"I just needed to sleep," I said. Dylan grimaced shaking his head. He glanced back at Levi and Nestor.

Nestor rose and said, "Come on, Levi. Let's go get some coffee and tell the nurses she's awake."

"Um, okay," he said with his eyes fixed on me.

The door clicked behind them, and Dylan sat on the edge of the bed. "I don't understand," I said.

"We almost lost you," he said.

"What? No, it's just a cold or the flu," I said thinking I'd become more human or something.

"It's not a sickness, Grace," he said. "It's a hex or a curse. Nestor could see it through his sight. We've called Jeremiah, but he hasn't responded. We need to call your father."

"No," I replied. The last thing I needed was my father, Oberon, to see me unable to complete my tasks here in Shady Grove. He would want to drag me back to the Otherworld.

"I think we should consider these nitwits wreaking havoc in town, ors someone is trying to kill you," he said. "You went to sleep in my arms at the store, but before I could get you here, you stopped breathing. Dr. Mistborne said that regular resuscitation techniques wouldn't work on you. She started some sort of fairy medicine with glowing crystals, and you started breathing again. You scared the shit out of me." As tears welled up in the corners of his eyes, he turned his face away from me.

"I'm sorry," I whispered.

He took the back of his hand and wiped the corners of his eyes. He cleared his throat, looking back at me, "Please let me call him."

"I'll call him," I said reluctantly. "Father, come forth." It only took a single request before he appeared.

A cool breeze flowed through the room, and a whirlwind of snow and ice coalesced into a tall man with dark features. He wore a light grey suit with a shimmering blue tie. "Gloriana, what are you doing in a human medical facility?" He asked with concern in his tone.

Father's minions had banished me to the human realm, but at some point, they decided to allow me to return to my father's world. I refused and stayed here. Since then I'd taken on the title Queen of the Exiles. My father approved of my choice, but we remained worlds apart.

"She's cursed or hexed or something," Dylan groaned.

Father raised his hand and shards of ice formed floating above his hand. Dylan looked alarmed, but I shook my head at him. The ice melted together into a slick reflecting oval. He looked through the double-sided mirror at me. Looking back at him, I could see his fairy features clearly. His ears were elongated to points. A diamond encrusted antler crown rose from his brow. His eyes were like sheets of pure glass with just the hint of blue. He closed his hand, and the ice shattered, but melted instantly. Dylan and I both flinched, but none of the shards reached us before they evaporated.

"Hexed," he replied. "Where is Deacon Giles?"

"Daddy, Deacon owns a farm here. The first menace actually attacked his livestock," I explained. "Deacon wouldn't hurt me."

"You are wrong. It is his time. It is Yule. His power grows daily. The closer you approach to the solstice the worse your condition will get. You must question him," he growled as his cold eyes stared at me. Father rarely showed any compassion, even for me.

"What is he?" Dylan asked my father. However, Daddy had said all he was going to say and faded back into nothingness. Dylan looked at me. "What is he?"

"Giles means goat," I said.

"He's Satan?" Dylan asked.

"No, not that terrible. He's not done anything wrong. Jeremiah made me aware of his presence, and I have since talked to him. He's just a farmer," I replied.

"Grace," he growled. "What is he?"

"Krampus," I replied quietly.

He stood up grabbing his jacket. "Stay here," he said.

"No, Dylan, don't bother Deacon. Please!" I pleaded.

"I'm going to kill him for hurting you," he growled slinging on his jacket.

"No, you aren't," I protested, pulling the blankets off my legs to get up.

"Grace, stay in that bed!" he yelled at me.

When I realized that he wouldn't relent, I used my last weapon, "He's under my protection as the Queen of the Exiles. I forbid you to touch him."

Rushing over toward me in anger, I shrank back from him to the edge of the bed. His eyes burned a blue flame. Reaching for me, I jerked away from him. As I started to fall off the back side of the bed, he wrapped his arms around my waist pulling me back to the bed. His muscles relaxed, but he breathed heavily.

Levi came in the door. "What's going on?"

"Get out, Levi," Dylan spoke monotone.

"Grace?" Levi asked me. I nodded my head. "Okay, I'm right outside."

"Dylan," I spoke his name as I traced his eyebrows with my cool fingers.

"You stopped breathing," he muttered.

"I know what that feels like," I said.

"And what did you do to the man that caused my death?" he asked.

"I made sure he paid for it," I replied knowing he spoke of Lysander, my former lawyer, not the actual man who pulled the trigger. "But, Darlin', Deacon didn't do this."

"You cannot know that for sure," he said, crawling up on the bed next to me. I was glad that his anger had subsided. The fire left his eyes, but I knew full well the panic he felt. I remembered the day I watched him die on a sidewalk in front of the county courthouse. Thankfully, Dylan had lied to me all those years about being human. Otherwise, he'd just be dead.

"Krampus is a horned deity worshiped by many pagans. Yes, the legends say that he stole the bad children and spanked them. Or ate them. But Deacon gains power from those who worship him. Witches for the most part. He didn't do this to me. He swore fealty to me when I visited him," I explained as he tightened his grip around my waist and molded his body to mine.

"Fealty?" he asked as his breath brushed over my hair.

"Complete loyalty. Breaking that would mean death," I said.

"Oh," he said. "Like an oath."

"Yes, his oath to abide by the rules we go by," I said.

"What rules?"

"We don't have anything official, but there are some givens. One of those is hexing the fairy queen," I replied smiling.

"We need a council," he said.

"Yes, we do. After Christmas, we can talk the mayor and see if he will let us have an election for the fairy council," I replied. "Are you okay?"

"Not really," he said slipping his warm hand into the split in the back of my hospital gown and resting it on the base of my back. "Just rest."

"Promise you will stay," I said.

"I promise," he replied without hesitation.

When I woke up, Dylan sat across the room in the chair staring at me. "Afternoon," he muttered.

"Now what's wrong?" I asked.

"Another brother," he said.

"What now?" I asked.

He rubbed his forehead signing. "Luther caught him at the diner. He said that he was sneaking in the backdoor stealing leftovers out of the refrigerator. Willie, his name is, explained that he was starving, but he only ate bites here and there. Like a taste test. He's at the jail with the rest."

I closed my eyes leaning back into the pillow. Dylan was beside me in an instant. He startled me, and I stared at him. "I'm still here. You will just have to endure me being alive," I joked.

He snarled pushing away from me. I'd played on his affections for too long. He loved me, and all I ever did was push him away. "Dylan, I'm sorry. Just trying to lighten the mood."

"Dr. Mistborne says you need to stay in bed. I'm going home to shower. I'll be back soon," he said, walking to the door.

"Please don't bother Deacon," I said suspecting that he intended to confront the horned deity.

Without turning to me, he said, "You asked me to leave him alone. I stayed here as you requested. Why don't you trust me? I know I lied about a lot of things, Grace. I don't know how to apologize anymore." Pulling the door open, he left the room without looking back.

As I laid in the dim room, tears flowed down my cheeks. I cursed myself for taking it too far.

Dr. Tabitha Mistborne entered the room with a smile, but it quickly faded. "How are you feeling?" She quickly scanned the room realizing I was alone.

"I've been better, but at the moment my body feels fine," I replied.

"So, the tears are for the handsome Mr. Riggs who is suspiciously absent?" she asked.

I shot her a look, but she pulled up a chair not fazed by my glare.

"Tell me what's going on," she demanded.

"I don't think that…" I stuttered.

"Whatever. Talk to me, Grace. Who are you going to talk to about it? Levi? Nestor? You sure as hell aren't talking to Dylan, so talk to me," she said. I knew I wasn't going to get her to go away. Actually, her direct manner was rather refreshing compared to everyone tip toeing around me.

"I need to get over the power trip, and just admit that…" I paused.

"That…" she prompted.

"That I love him," I said.

She smiled satisfied with my admission. "Was that so hard?"

"You aren't him," I said. "Can you reverse this curse or is it going to kill me?"

"Honestly, I don't know," she said. "All I am doing is responding to your symptoms."

"I need to go talk to Deacon," I said.

"You shouldn't leave. Send Dylan," she suggested.

"I don't know if he's coming back," I admitted.

"Whatever. He is addicted to you. He's coming back," she assured me.

"Are you forcing me to stay?" I asked.

"No, but you need to stay. Just my advice," she said.

I pushed myself up out of the bed, and Dr. Mistborne helped me get dressed.

As I stepped into the parking lot, I realized Dylan was back. His red Camaro was parked in the front row. Walking towards it, I saw two figures wrapped around each other intimately. The silhouette of the female sat astride the driver. I stepped backwards clasping my hands over my mouth. A small sob escaped my lips. I waited too long. This was my own fault.

How could he have turned away from me so quickly? Perhaps the bond I thought we had was something only I felt. Perhaps I had carried it all too far. "Dylan," his name escaped my lips as a whimper.

The car rocked in a swaying motion. Stepping backwards, I moved slowly away in shock. I pulled my cell phone out to call Levi to pick me up. My hands shook causing me to drop the phone.

I reached down to pick it up as my heart pounded in my throat.

"Grace!" Looking up I met, Dylan's eyes as he exited the med center. I turned back to his car in confusion. It continued to rock. Squatting in the middle of the parking lot, I shifted eyes back and forth. Vaguely, I saw Dylan running to me before a flash of head-lights and a searing pain erupted in my head as it made contact with a chrome bumper.

6

DECEMBER 17TH

I WOKE UP ON A COLD METAL SLAB WITH BRIGHT FLUORESCENCE IN the room. Wiping my eyes, I rose up realizing the reason it was cold was because I was naked on the metal table.

Looking down at my arm where the tattoo that stored my power stained my otherwise flawless skin, I expected to see the dark red jewel and black filigree. However, it glimmered in silver light. The heart stone flashed a sapphire blue. Reaching up to my hair, my vision focused on platinum locks. "Gloriana," I muttered.

A man entered the room, then screamed like a girl. "You are alive!" he exclaimed. He reached to pull out a cell phone as I stared at him and the lettering in the door behind him. Morgue.

"Shi-yat! Where is Dylan Riggs?" I shouted at the stunned man.

He muttered into the phone, "She's not dead. Get down here." He hung up trembling.

I heard running footsteps, and Levi burst into the room. He stopped,grg gawking at me. I grabbed the sheet folded on the table next to me throwing it over my naked body. He rushed up throwing his arms around me.

"I thought you were gone," he whispered in my ear. He shook as he pulled back to meet my eyes.

"I died?"

"They tried to bring you back for hours," he muttered. Then he kissed me on the cheek. "Grace, don't leave me."

I returned his embrace. My emotional bard. "I'm not going anywhere."

"How are you still here?"

"I use a lot of power to look like Grace. When I'm like this, I've got a lot more power, but a lot less control. The glamour of Grace is not only just a look, but a binding on wild fairy powers. However, it's that power that makes me immortal. I suppose, it's what's keeping me alive. Levi, just be prepared to stop me, if it comes to that," I said.

He nodded, but grimaced knowing what I was asking him to do.

"What's going on with you and Kady?"

He laughed. "You just woke up in the morgue, and you are asking me about my girlfriend. Well, ex-girlfriend."

"Oh, no," I muttered. "What happened?"

"She said that she was tired of playing second fiddle," he muttered.

"Levi, are you cheating on her?" I asked.

"No, she meant you," he said cautiously.

"You informed her that you and I aren't together, right?"

"Multiple times, but you've been sick. I wanted to stay here with you, and she got mad. She doesn't understand our relationship," he said.

"Well, I'm not your mother," I said.

"Definitely not," he said.

"Not a sister or cousin," I continued.

"No," he said as his grip tightened around my waist. The thin sheet wasn't much of a barrier between us.

"How about a best friend?" I suggested.

"With benefits?" he smirked.

"No!" I laughed at him.

"I'll try that with her. Maybe she will listen," he said.

"Where is he?" I finally asked.

"Oh shit, Grace, he went after Deacon," he said.

"Help me up," I said. He backed off the edge of the table steadying me as I stood.

"I need juice," I said feeling depleted.

He rolled up his sleeve, revealing the Celtic knotwork tattoo on his arm. While teaching him to use his basic magic skills over the past few months, we realized that he could store power like I did, but we could also swap power back and forth. He called it swapping gravy, because he knew how much I got a kick out of his favorite euphemism for sex, locking legs and swapping gravy. He embarrassed me every time he said it.

I ran my pale cool hand over his tattoo, and my head whipped back as I pulled power from him to me. Storing it in the blue jewel on my arm, the ecstasy of the tendrils of power pulsed into every part of my body. Involuntary, I pressed my body to his.

"Grace, that's enough," he said as the force of his magic powered by his will slammed into me. I released my grip. The cold fairy in me squealed with the delight of drinking in power from him.

No matter how many times we practiced sharing power, the recipient always drifted on the edge of an erotic experience. I grimaced.

"Sorry," I muttered.

"It was good for me, what about you?" he teased, but quickly sobered. "We need to find a way to do that without the foreplay or Dylan is going to kill me."

"I agree," I replied. "Help me outside so I can shift us to Deacon's farm." Before we left the morgue, I used power to clothe myself in the long silver dress I normally wore in this state.

Levi helped me outside and made our way to the nearest oak. "Let me handle him. He's going to be pissed."

"Who was in his car in the parking lot?" I asked remembering the couple in the Camaro.

"That wasn't his car, Grace. One of the city councilmen just bought one. I think it was him," he said.

"Fucking fairies," I muttered.

He nodded as I put my hand on the oak. The old tree spoke to me, warning me of tension near the sight I requested to make a way. I thanked the tree as I opened the way. As Levi and I stepped through, I saw Dylan throwing haymakers at Deacon Giles. Deacon dodged him, begging him to stop. A trickle of blood rolled out of his nose where Dylan had made contact at some point.

Dylan's searing anger rippled off him in waves of heat. The atmosphere outside Deacon's farmhouse was soupy like the dead of summer.

Forcing power and my will through my voice, I spoke, "Enough!" As the tingling sensation of magic wound itself around my limbs and vibrated through my chest. My skin illuminated as the filigree from my tattoo swirled up my arm, then across my chest.

Dylan's coiled form stopped mid-punch. Turning toward my voice, his burning eyes fixed on me. Deacon hit his knees, hiding his face. Frost stretched from the hem of my dress toward the two men before me.

Slowly I approached Dylan whose face was blank. No emotion. I couldn't tell if he was mad or shocked. As I moved closer, tracks of tears glistened on his cheeks. Stopping several feet from him, confusion finally registered on his face.

"Grace?"

"Dylan Riggs, you will not harm my servant," I spoke realizing that the fairy queen in me had an agenda.

"Grace?" he muttered again. The blue flames in his eyes settled. As he stepped toward me, I threw my hands up.

"Don't touch me," I warned.

"How? You were gone. She said you were gone."

"Apparently, Gloriana is hard to kill," I spoke of myself in the third person because the ice queen within me was a being I'd tried to suppress, but as the power flowed through me I knew she was the only thing keeping me alive. "If you touch me, I might melt. Please don't."

He nodded understanding. "Is the curse still there?"

"It is, but I can control it better this way," I said.

The fire returned to his eyes. "You!" he growled at Deacon.

"I swear on my life. I have not cursed the Queen," Deacon defended himself from his prostrate position.

"Your father said…," Dylan started.

"Father hates Deacon for good reason. Deacon was a very bad fairy before getting kicked out of the Otherworld. I don't think he's directly behind my curse. However, I do believe he knows something that may help us. Deacon please stand and speak with me."

Climbing off his knees, Deacon Giles stood before me in denim overalls and a long sleeve flannel shirt. He brushed off his pants rising to full height. He was well over six foot tall. He could have smashed Dylan like a bug, if he'd changed into the half-goat, half-demon form of Krampus.

"How may I serve you, my Queen?"

"My father suggested that you might have something to do with this death curse," I accused him.

"I would never do anything to harm you. I swore my fealty," he said.

Taking several steps toward him, I stood close to the still stunned Dylan Riggs. It took everything I had not to reach out to him. Once before his abilities as a Phoenix forced me out of the ice queen facade. However, if he touched me now while suppressing this power, I wasn't sure I would be able to control the curse as Grace.

"You are the horned god, worshipped by covens across the world. Perhaps a coven requested a death curse that you granted," I suggested.

His dark eyes flickered with recollection. "I granted a death curse to a Cane Creek Coven 4 days ago," he admitted. "They didn't call you by name."

"Lisette," Levi muttered behind me. He'd been so quiet that I'd forgotten he was there.

Dylan's breathing increased again, and his knuckles popped as he clinched his fists.

"Deacon, maybe in the future you should require a name before you grant curses," I suggested holding back a snarl.

"I offer my life," he said producing a long machete from his pants. He had fought Dylan hand to hand never drawing the weapon. He nudged the weapon to me. I crossed my arms, shaking my head. He offered it to Dylan. I refused to look at him to allow him to make a decision. Dylan turned his back on him.

"Can you reverse the curse?" I asked. My knowledge of curses and hexes was limited to placing them, not removing them.

"No. However, the curse draws power as I do until the solstice. If you can fight it until then, it will fade away," he explained.

"Three days," I muttered. "You will change your policies, Krampus! Do you understand?"

His form shifted as I spoke his true name. Two long twisted curling horns rose from his head, and his feet turned to hooves. His nose elongated making his mouth a hairy snout with slender, sharp teeth. Dylan and Levi both jumped in front of me. I chuckled at the chivalry, but a warm feeling rushed over my heart. I rarely felt my heart beat in the cold state, but it thumped hard.

The goat man knelt on one knee. "I will do as you request, my Queen."

"Very well, we take our leave," I said turning to the gravel driveway at the farm. Dylan's red Camaro sat there with the driver's door open. As I approached it, he stepped up next to me.

"Are you okay?" he asked.

"No. Are you?" I returned.

"Not at all," he said.

"Levi, I'm going to shift you back to the trailer. We will meet you there."

"You sure?" he asked.

I touched his cheek. "Thank you, my dear bard. I am sure." Dylan leered at my hand, knowing that he couldn't touch me.

I touched the tree we arrived through and requested that it send Levi home. It obliged me sending Levi home the moment he touched it.

Dylan opened the passenger door for me as I gathered my dress to take a seat. I slid down into the leather seat and breathed in Dylan's scent. My senses were always heightened in this form. I loved the familiar mix of leather, peppermint and musk.

He jumped in speeding away. As I looked in the side mirror, Deacon Giles had shifted back into his farmers clothes, and walked toward the house.

Once we reached the main road back to town, Dylan spoke. "Shouldn't you go back to the hospital?"

"Did that car hit me?" I asked.

"You don't remember?"

"Bright lights and searing pain," I said.

"Yes," he muttered.

"I woke up in the morgue," I said.

He jerked the car to the side of the road, cutting off the ignition. He gripped the steering wheel.

"I never imagined I'd feel such pain. You died right there on the pavement, but Dr. Mistborne fought to bring you back for hours. At some point, she gave up. I wanted to kill something. Forgive me for going after him," he said.

"No," I said flatly.

"I know I promised, but Grace…"

I waved my hand at him, because he'd misunderstood. "You were right. He was involved. I'm not angry with you."

"You've been angry with me since I returned," he muttered.

"I was never mad, just afraid," I said. His eyes met mine as he groaned.

"And now I can't touch you," he complained.

"Three days isn't so long," I said.

"Feels like an eternity," he said. "Levi can touch you. It isn't fair!" he whined.

I giggled at him and dared to tease. "Yes, he even loaned me power."

"You swapped gravy with that son of a bitch!" he said, as the killer smile appeared.

I laughed, "I did. It was wonderful."

"I always knew you wanted him," he said.

"I want you both," I pushed the tease.

"No."

"No?"

"No, you are mine, and I am yours," he said as his eyes smoldered.

"Yes, but we've both got to stop dying."

"I agree," he said. "So, I can't touch you?"

"You want to take the chance?"

He groaned, "No."

Sitting next to Dylan at the bar, Nestor served us both a cup of his decadent coffee. It eased my nerves. Dylan also visibly relaxed, but I keenly felt the radiant heat of his body. The cold I felt wanted it. This was torture.

"Thanks, Nestor," he muttered.

Levi spent most of the day flipping through websites on the laptop computer he had recently bought. He was sure he could google enough things to find out who these brothers actually were.

"I think we should go to the jail, confront them, and demand them to tell us who they are," I said.

"You are not going anywhere near them," he said. "This all started when they came to town."

"Yes, but Deacon said this was the witches, not the goof ball brothers," I replied.

"Perhaps let Levi go talk to them. It will be a good exercise for his magic development. See what he can find out from them. They are harmless, mostly," Nestor offered.

"Where is he?" Dylan asked.

"He went to meet Kady at the diner for dinner, and to talk to Luther about the one they caught stealing food," I said. "We can send him to the jail afterwards. He and Kady are fighting."

"About what?" Dylan asked.

I sipped my coffee and didn't answer. Nestor stopped drying glasses, waiting for my answer.

"She has some reservations about his relationship with me," I tried putting it delicately.

"What relationship?" Dylan asked.

"That's just it, we don't have one. Other than he lives with me, and we get along very well. She thinks I'm a threat, I guess," I said.

"I can understand that," Dylan said.

"Do you think Levi is a threat to us?" I asked.

"Is there an us?" Dylan asked.

Nestor cleared his throat and walked to the end of the bar to talk to one of the patrons that came in during the lunch hour. The bar opened around lunch and stayed open well into the night. Occasionally, Nestor would have a rush at lunch. However, today there were only three other people in the bar besides Dylan, Nestor and me.

I looked him in the eye. "You know there is," I replied. The last twelve hours were the longest I've spent in fairy form since I compartmentalized Gloriana ages ago. One of the things I'd forgotten about was that she couldn't lie. Dylan hadn't picked up on it yet, but he knew something was different. I'd never lied to him, but I'd certainly hidden my feelings. Gloriana was an open book.

"When you go back to being Grace, are you going to admit that?" he asked.

"I am Grace, Dylan."

"I know, but you are so different like this. Honest," he said.

Okay, so he had picked up on it. Once a lawman, always a lawman.

"Well, Detective Riggs, perhaps I am a bit different, but I'm still me," I said.

"Prove it," he said.

"Fuck off," I said.

He laughed, "Yes, you are still Grace. Vulgar mouth."

"Too bad you can't touch me, I'd love to show you how vulgar," I teased.

"Good grief! Stop!" he begged.

Across the room, a loud clatter caught our attention. Nestor was wrestling across the bar with one of the patrons. Dylan sprinted to aid him. I approached cautiously. The beady eyed man, clearly inebriated, played tug of war with Nestor over a bowl of nuts. It was the same man I'd seen in the bar a couple of days ago when Levi put up the decorations.

Along the bar, Nestor had bowls of mixed nuts for the patrons to munch on. Sometimes he had pretzels and other snacks too. But today, it was just nuts, and the angry man, clearly a brother, tried wrenching the bowl from Nestor's grip. Once Dylan joined the fray, the patron released his grip and went flying backwards off the stool into the floor.

"My Queen, have mercy," he screamed.

"Somebody kill me now," I said.

"Grace!" Dylan spouted. I supposed my choice of words was inappropriate.

I waved him off. "Get up you fool!" I ordered the half-drunk man. If he was completely drunk, he wouldn't have the wits to know who I was, much less speak.

"I just wanted the bowl. I mean no harm," he said.

"My bowls have been going missing all week," Nestor admitted.

"Have you been stealing bowls all week?" I asked.

"Yes, ma'am," he lowered his head in shame.

"What's your name?" I asked.

"Chad," he replied.

"Well, Chadwick, you are going down to the jail to spend some quality time with your brothers," I replied.

"Yeah, I know several of them got pinched," he replied.

"How many brothers do you have?" I asked.

"Twelve," he replied.

"Holy hell," Dylan muttered. "Seven more."

I laughed. Picking up my cell phone, I called Levi.

"Hey, Grace, what's wrong?" he asked immediately.

"You still having lunch with Kady?" I asked.

"No, she left earlier," he said.

"Get over here to the bar. I've got some info for your internet search," I said. "And bring me a chocolate milkshake."

"As you wish, my Queen. I'm on my way," he replied and hung up.

"I'll call Troy to come pick this one up," Dylan said stepping away.

"Get up and sit on this stool," I told the beady eyed fellow. He obeyed and propped himself up at the bar. "Can I have more peanuts?"

"No," growled Nestor. I chuckled.

"Pretty sure you burned that bridge, Chad," I said.

"Darn," he replied.

"Do all of your brothers steal things?" I asked.

"No, Lamar likes to tip cows," he replied.

"Yes, I met Lamar," I said. "Why are you in Shady Grove?"

"Our mother is supposed to meet us here for Christmas. We

have discussed moving here with your permission, of course," he said.

"I don't decide who stays. However, if you steal things and torture animals, I'll kick you out of town. Or end you, whichever is easier," I said.

He gulped, "That would be unfortunate."

"It's a matter of perspective," I replied. "You and your brothers are a menace. I don't have time for you."

"Yeah, because you are dying," he said.

"What!" Dylan said, suddenly hanging up the phone. "What did you say?"

"She's dying. She's cursed," he said.

"How do you know that?" I asked him.

"My mother does magic. She taught us how to recognize it. Unfortunately, for you, you might not be around to end us," he said without hatred.

"Who is your mother?" I asked.

"I'll introduce you when she arrives," he said.

"What is her name?" I pressed.

"She doesn't allow us to speak it," he said.

Levi entered the bar. The cool air from outside rushed into the bar as he closed the door behind him. "If I didn't know better, I'd say it was going to snow."

"It's Alabama. It doesn't snow here," Nestor said.

I turned to him. "Oh really?" As Levi stuck the chocolate shake in my hand. I took a long sip of it staring at Dylan.

"Fuck," I heard him mutter as he turned away.

"You can do that?" Levi asked.

"Yes, but I don't. Last thing I need is attention for creating a freak snow storm," I replied.

"Who's this?" Levi asked.

"Levi, meet Chad. Chad, Levi," I introduced them as I enjoyed more chocolate shake. Dylan watched me too intently, cutting his eyes away when I looked up at him.

"What did you find out?" Levi asked me while eyeballing him.

"He has 12 brothers," I said. "Thanks for the shake. It's delicious." I licked my lips.

"Oh, okay," he said finally realizing I was teasing Dylan. He gulped as he plopped down on a stool. He pulled out his phone and started searching. Nestor sat a cup of coffee in front of him, but he didn't acknowledge it. I poked him in the side as I pointed at the coffee. "Oh, thanks Nestor."

"You are welcome, Levi," Nestor responded keeping his eyes on Chad.

Dylan came up behind Levi and watched him search. "You are breathing down my neck," Levi said.

"Sorry," Dylan muttered. He picked up his cup of coffee downing the rest of it in one sip. He fixed his eyes on me waiting for me to enjoy more of the shake. He nodded toward it. It made me giggle.

"Staring is rude. You begged me to stop torturing you. I'm just enjoying this chocolate shake," I said wrapping my lips around the straw.

"Staring is all I can do, for now, but you will pay for it. Keep it up, Blondie," Nestor refilled his cup offering him the sugar. Dylan spooned two helpings into the cup and turned to Levi. "Levi, what does the Wizard of Google say?"

"Looks like they are Yule Lads," he said.

Chad gasped. "Thanks for the confirmation bowl thief," I said to him.

"It's not what you think!" he protested.

"I think you and your brothers are in my town causing havoc right before a huge holiday celebration. Aren't Christmas elves supposed to bring toys and goodies?" I asked.

"He's not an elf. He's a troll," Levi said.

Chad started giggling. My anger rose as I approached him. He saw me coming and stopped laughing. I thought about how each one of his brothers were interrupting my holiday. The curse was weighing on me, and I just wanted to have a holiday with my family. Was it too much to ask? I intended to take it out on him.

"You son of a bitch!"

"Don't talk about my mother that way," he yelled but slid off the stool moving away from me.

"Grace, leave him be," Dylan said.

"No, he and his brothers are interfering with our town. With my town. I'm done with it. I'm not here for his amusement!" I said stalking toward him.

"Levi, get her," Dylan growled.

"Huh?" Levi muttered, his attention still on his phone search. Dylan grabbed him by the collar and shoved him toward me. "Oh, Grace, stop!"

"He's going to pay," I said ignoring them. Cold gripped my heart as the tattoo on my right arm ignited. A battle waged inside of me. I was the Queen of the Exiles. This was my town. This twirp and his brothers were causing a disaster. Gloriana was keeping me alive, but she was also in control. It was like watching a train wreck while driving the train.

Levi grabbed me by the waist. I wrestled with him, but I knew his ability to control me. Plus, he was damn strong. "Stop it, Grace," he forced his will through his voice. I stopped struggling with him and stood still. He released his hold on my waist, so I spun shoving him across the room.

Dylan sprinted across the room standing between me and Chad. "You will stop," he said.

"You can't touch me," I said.

"I can. I just don't want to do it," he said.

"Oh, you don't want to touch me," I purred. I still had the milk-shake. Bringing it to my lips, I stared at him.

He stammered, "I mean, I do want to, but I…"

I paced right in front of him. "But what, my love?"

The bar door slammed open once again. Sheriff Troy Maynard

entered. "Hey everybody, where's the new menace?" He stopped and stared at us. "What's going on?"

"Stupefy," Levi said softly in my ear, and my knees buckled. He caught me before I hit the floor. Dylan ran his hand through his hair turning his back to me. He'd been distracting me as Levi approached. Levi deposited me in a chair near the pool table. I tried to cuss him, but my mouth felt like jelly. "You can beat me within an inch of my life later," he muttered before leaving me sitting there.

He and Dylan explained to Troy the situation. "Thirteen!" he exclaimed. "I don't have room for thirteen prisoners!"

"We don't take up much room. Back home we shared one room," Chad replied. "We were kind of poor."

"Shut up!" Dylan said.

"We will figure something out," Troy said. "What should we expect with the next one?"

"According to the article online, the next one slams doors," Levi said.

The troll laughed. "Hee hee! Ol' Keith! He's a pistol!"

"Shut up!" Dylan shouted again.

I'd regained my ability to walk and talk, but I didn't clue them into it. However, Nestor walked over, took the milkshake which was mostly gone, and handed me my coffee cup refilled.

"Drink," he said.

I looked down at it and could tell he'd altered the spell inside the coffee. It normally had floating glitter in its muddy darkness, however this one had an oil slick sheen to it. "What did you do to it?"

"Drink," he replied, walking away. I took several sips and previously his coffee would warm the soul. I supposed he didn't want to take chances with warming me up. The coffee just tasted good and my senses heightened beyond their already sensitive state. Look at all of them, I could visibly see the stress on Dylan and Levi. They both cringed at the moment Troy would haul Chad away giving me the chance to exact my wrath on them for subduing me.

The truth was I'd always avoided being the fairy queen, because I didn't always have control over the impulses that came with being that part of myself. I was working on a full-fledged multiple personality disorder. Perhaps I should go visit the local shrink, Dr. Deon Tucker.

Levi was my anchor. The bard that could control me. Dylan's grip on my heart reached through the cold exterior warming me without a touch. I didn't need a shrink. I had my own rescue squad. Look down at the coffee, I swirled it around and the spell faded. When I lifted my eyes, Nestor watched me. I nodded to him, and he smiled.

Troy left with the troll. My two men turned to face my wrath. I stood and walked to the bar ignoring them. Setting my cup down on the counter, I said, "Thank you, Nestor."

"Grace, I had to," Levi said. When I turned to look at them both, Dylan elbowed him in the ribs. I wasn't sure what that was about, but it made me laugh.

"Get over yourselves. I'm not mad," I said. "Stupefy? Really Levi? You've been playing fantasy card games again, haven't you?" He blushed, because I knew his nerdy little secret. He'd started playing one of those silly card games with guys he met at church. Levi Rearden was no nerd. He was sex on a stick, but he'd made quick friends with the awkward crowd.

"You aren't mad?" Dylan asked.

"No, but I suggest you don't try your luck, Pookie," I responded.

"Oh, hell no!" he exclaimed.

"What? You said you needed a nickname!" I reminded him.

"Not that!" he said.

"Pookie," Levi giggled. Dylan elbowed him again.

"Grace," Dylan growled.

"Well, if you don't like it, perhaps you should think of something else," I suggested.

"I was thinking Stud," he grinned.

"Keep dreaming, Dylan," I said.

"How about Sexy Beast?" he said.

"I really like Pookie," I replied.

"You better not!" he said.

"Methinks you protest too much. That you secretly like it," I teased.

Levi continued to laugh. I even heard Nestor smirk behind the bar. "Play me for it," he said nodded toward the pool table.

"Oh, a rematch," I grinned

"If you win, you can call me Pookie or whatever you want," he said. "If I win, I pick my own nickname."

"You cheated last time," I said.

"No, Nestor cheated," he claimed.

"Leave me out of it," Nestor interjected.

"When was this?" Levi asked.

"A long, long time ago," I laughed.

Dylan said, "Long ago as in four months. So, are you scared, Fairy Queen?"

"I told you once before that calling me a coward doesn't faze me, Dylan Riggs," I said.

"No, it doesn't, but you still want to play," he said.

"Nestor, I'm going to need tequila," I said.

He promptly poured two shots.

"What the hell?" Levi said.

"Sit down and watch," I told him as he slid onto one of the bar stools. I stared at Dylan as I licked my wrist pouring salt over it. He shook his head. I licked it again downing the first shot quickly.

"Wow," Levi said staring at me.

"Rack 'em up, Pookie," I said.

He pulled the rack off the wall arranging the balls in the staggered order. Drawing on the power in my tattoo, I shifted my shimmering gown to the silver duplicate of my outfit the night I first played pool with Dylan Riggs. As he looked up from the rack, he gulped. Raising my eyebrows at him, I said, "Trying to make it authentic."

"Holy shit," Levi said. Walking up to him, I remembered the poor blokes who lined the stools that night. I ran a fingernail up his arm. He shivered.

"My dear Levi, Mr. Riggs and I played this game once before and he cheated," I said with his eyes fixed on mine.

"Uh-huh," Levi muttered as Nestor laughed.

"Dylan won the game," I said. Dylan's eyes blazed as I touched Levi.

"What did he win?" Levi asked in a whisper as I stood close to his ear.

"A kiss," I replied.

"It was more than that," Dylan interjected.

"It was? Oh, oh, OH!" Levi said realizing the significance.

"I did everything I could to distract him. Showed my boobs. Shook my booty, but alas, Sheriff Dylan Riggs had game," I said.

"I don't believe that at all," Levi smirked.

"Get over here and break, Grace," Dylan said fed up with the tease already.

"No, you go ahead, Pookie. You won't beat me this time," I said.

"Fine," he said lining up his shot. He broke the balls apart. None fell. "Damnit."

"Bad time to lose your touch, Honey Bunny," I said.

He groaned. "I think Pookie was better."

Lining up shot after shot, I dropped four balls in a row missing the fifth by a millimeter.

"Your turn, Puddin'," I said motioning to the table.

He shook his head, but quickly honed in sinking ball after ball. He had one stripe, plus the eight remaining. He missed the shot on the stripe.

"Poor Muffin," I cooed. Levi and Nestor laughed. I slammed down the second shot. No salt. It had been so long since I'd had any alcohol, the tart burn made me shudder.

Finishing off the table except for the eight, I lined up the shot leaning over the table and winking at my victim. "Get on with it," he grumped.

"Now, now, Mr. Riggs, no bitterness," I teased.

I struck the white ball sucking in a small breath causing it to backspin and slow down. It rolled to balance on the edge of the pocket. Perfect.

As it teetered on the edge, Levi stood approaching it cautiously. "It's not falling," he said.

"Well, darn, it's your table, Boo Bear," I nodded to Dylan.

He grabbed his stick, dropping his last ball before even lining it up. He eyed the shot on the eight ball, then stared at me.

"What did you do to it?" he asked.

"Whatever do you mean, Snuggle Bumpkin?"

He grinned. "You did something to it. There is no way you missed that shot."

"Are you accusing me of throwing the game, Gum Drop?" I acted innocent.

"Yes, I am," he said.

"How dare you, Love Bug! I thought we had something," I grinned.

He pointed the stick at me and said, "After this shot, you've got to stop with the names!"

"As you wish, Sugar Lips," I grinned.

"That's my favorite," Levi said. It was the best one so far. I could always taste the sugar from Dylan's coffee on his lips.

"Shut up, Levi!" Dylan said.

He lined up the shot, and the eight ball fell easily. Leaning on the stick, he seemed quite satisfied with himself.

"What shall it be, Mr. Riggs?" I asked grinning.

He placed the stick on the table and rolled it across the felt. Stalking toward my position at the edge of the bar, he leaned on it with arms on either side of me careful not to touch me. He leaned into my ear, whispering the name. When he backed away, I stared at him and nodded.

"Seems kinda plain," I said.

"I like the way it rolls across your lips," he said.

"What is it?" Levi asked enthralled with the whole conversation.

"Shut it, Levi," Dylan said staring at me. "Well?"

"You won fair and square," I replied.

"Say it," he prompted.

"Not here," I pretended to be shy.

"Say it. I won, Grace," he said.

"I let you win," I protested.

"Did you?" he asked. "You cheated?"

"No, you can't cheat to lose!" I said.

"I put nothing past you in this form!" he replied. "I don't know why you let me win, other than you knew good and well, I had no intention to let you call me Pookie or some other asinine name."

"Pookie is such a sweet name," I said grabbing his shirt. He flinched at the contact. I was sure not to touch his skin, but even touching his shirt, I could feel the heat radiating off his body.

"Let go. Please," he said nervously. The fear of losing me broke through the game, so I released him, but leaned forward and whispered the name he'd requested.

I leaned back watching his eyes roll back in his head. How ridiculous! Over a pet name.

"No more milkshakes," he grinned.

"You can't handle it," I replied.

"No, I can't," he admitted.

"I can't hear y'all. What are y'all saying?" Levi teased.

"I thought I told you to shut up, Levi?!" Dylan said.

Levi lifted his hands in surrender. "It can't be as good as Dublin," he muttered. I agreed, but it was what he wanted. I was to the point where I'd give him whatever he wanted.

7

DECEMBER 18TH

THE CALL CAME WHILE LEVI AND I MADE COOKIES WITH WINNIE.

We'd cut out Christmas shapes, decorating them with sprinkles. We were waiting on them to finish while Dylan watched television.

"I'm so excited," Winnie jumped up and down shaking the whole trailer.

"Calm down, munchkin. You are shaking the whole house," I said.

"It's a trailer, Aunt Grace. Not a house," she corrected me.

"Well, haven't you developed a smart mouth!" I said. "If you are naughty, Santa Claus won't come."

"Momma said Santa Claus wasn't coming this year anyway," she said.

"What? Why not?" Levi asked.

"She said he didn't come to the poor houses," she said without a hint of disappointment. She'd accepted that there would be no presents.

"That's not true," Dylan said. "I talked to him yesterday, Winnie. He told me he was excited to bring your gifts."

"Mr. Dylan wouldn't lie," Winnie said looking at me.

"No, sweetheart, he wouldn't," I said. At least not to her.

"Yay! I'm sorry for my smart mouth, Aunt Grace! I want Santa to come," she said. She went over to Dylan on the couch and told him what she wanted for Christmas so he could tell Santa the next time he talked to him.

"I can't believe Bethany told her that," Levi growled.

"Bethany isn't right in the head most of the time. She *is* poor. I always make sure Winnie gets a visit from Santa. Bethany protests when I bring the toys over after dark. But this last time, I told her that I never wanted to hear her complain about it again. Apparently, she and I need to revisit the discussion," I said.

"Probably best you don't do that now," Levi suggested.

"You are right. You go tell her," I said.

"I think I will. Only she has a visitor at the moment," he said.

"Fucking whore," I muttered.

"Grace," Dylan warned. Sometimes I thought he had super hearing. I wanted to reintroduce him to my middle finger, but I just turned my back.

Levi joined them sitting in my recliner. My cell phone rang as they spoke.

"Hello," I answered.

"Miss Bryant, this is Deon Tucker. I have a patient here that I think you should come and speak to, if you could," he said.

"What's his name?" I asked.

"Keith," he replied.

"How did I know?" I smirked.

"Pardon," Deon said.

"I'm sorry, Dr. Tucker. Just call Sheriff Maynard to come and get him," I replied.

Dylan's eyes turned from Winnie to me. I shook my head.

"He's pretty insistent on talking to you. He's here for an anger management session, but he says he won't do it until he talks to you," the doctor informed me as I heard a door slam.

"What was that?" I asked.

"He just stormed out," he said.

"Call the sheriff. Tell him what happened. We knew that Keith would be next on our list," I said.

"What list?" he asked.

"Trolls. He's a troll," I said.

"Oh, okay," he replied. "I'll call Sheriff Maynard."

"Thanks," I said hanging up the phone.

"An angry troll just left Dr. Tucker's office," I explained to Dylan and Levi.

"I'll go see if I can track him," Dylan said grabbing his jacket.

"You don't have to go. Let Troy handle it," I said.

"Troy's hands are full. I need to help," he said.

"You don't have to rescue everyone. You aren't the sheriff anymore," I protested.

"I know that, Grace. Thank you for reminding me," he said storming out the front door.

I followed him into the yard. "I'm sorry, Dylan. I know that's my fault that you aren't the sheriff. I'm sorry. Please don't leave mad."

He stopped, putting his hands on his hips. It lifted up his jacket giving me a nice view of his ass. I forgot about his anger and stared at it.

"I don't blame you, Grace," he said jarring me back to reality.

"Oh, hum. Okay," I stammered.

He turned to look at me. I blushed looking away. "Were you staring at my butt?" he asked.

"It was right there! How could I not?" I said.

He quirked a smile climbing in his car, "I'll be back soon. I know you'll miss my ass."

"I got my fill for now," I said.

He laughed as he shut the door, firing the red Camaro up. Pulling out of the drive, he waved to me as I watched him exit the trailer park heading toward Main Street.

As I returned to Levi and Winnie, she was now telling Levi what all she wanted for Christmas. I checked on the cookies, pulling them out to cool.

"Oh! Are they ready?" Winnie asked.

"Yes ma'am, but they have to cool before we can eat any of them," I explained.

"I want a snowflake with some milk," she proclaimed. "What kind do you want, Uncle Levi?"

"I think I'll have a Christmas tree," he replied.

"What about you, Aunt Grace?" she asked.

"I want a phoenix," I said.

"Gross," Levi said.

"You just wish I'd said a bard!" I replied.

"Well, no, but maybe," he blushed. Damn that was adorable.

"What's a phoenix?" Winnie asked not missing anything.

"It's a bird," I replied.

"Not any birds like that around here," she said. Levi laughed.

"I'll have a candy cane cookie," I said drawing her attention away from the bird.

"With milk?" she asked.

"With milk," I confirmed.

Dylan returned that afternoon with the story of chasing the door slammer through the doctor's office complex near the med center. He enjoyed cookies at Winnie's insistence. We laughed at all the nonsense involved. The troll kept demanding to see me.

"He said that he had to get you before his brother did," Dylan said.

"Which one?" I asked.

"He didn't say. Of course, by that time, I had him on the ground as Troy cuffed him," he said. "He was stronger than Phil."

"He slammed every door in the building multiple times. Like he had a door fetish," Dylan said.

"What's a fetish?" Winnie asked.

Dylan's eyes widened as the color drained from his face. I held back a laugh.

67

"I'm not touching that one," Levi said.

"Fetish is a word that little girls who want presents from Santa Claus does not say," I said.

"Oh," Winnie replied thinking about my answer. "But what is it?"

"Never you mind," I said pushing her toward the bathroom to wash her hands for dinner.

"Sorry," Dylan muttered. "She picks up on everything!"

"I know. I've let a few slip in front of her," I admitted. "But that one is a doozy."

Levi made a pot of stew from a Yule recipe he found online, and we enjoyed it along with more cookies.

"What's the next brother?" I asked.

"This one is weird. He eats yogurt," he said.

"I guess we should watch for him at the Food Mart," I said.

"That would be logical, but I'm thinking it won't be that easy," Levi said.

"You are probably right," I replied.

"Alright, Winnie, are you staying here tonight or are you going home?" I asked her.

She snuggled up next to Levi and said, "I'm staying here."

"Are you afraid to go home?" I asked.

"Yes, mommy acts weird sometimes," she said.

I felt bad because Winnie was getting old enough to understand when her mother wasn't right. "Sure, you can stay here," I said.

Levi scooped her up taking her to the front bedroom. She giggled as he tossed her up in the air.

"I wish there was a way to convince Bethany to let her stay with you all the time," Dylan said.

"You think the vulgar mouth fairy queen is better than her mother?" I asked.

"Yes," he said. "Infinitely better."

"You would help me with her?" I asked.

68

The smile that always weakened my knees crossed his face, "Yes, of course."

"You would make a good father," I said.

He sat down in my recliner and leaned back. "I've never thought of having children."

"Never?" I asked. "Why not? You have to have an heir."

"Yeah, I know. To be honest, I have been pretty negligent in the heir department. Never found the right mother," he said watching my reaction.

As I leaned on the kitchen counter, my platinum locks swept down my cheek in front of my face. I pushed them away locking eyes with Dylan. "You can't possibly mean me," I said.

"Why not?" he asked.

"Look at me. I'm a mess. Half fairy queen, half trailer trash. I'm not exactly ideal mother material," I said.

He leaned up in the chair, sitting on the edge. "I see the way you are with Winnie, and I know that if anything ever happened to Bethany, you would take her. In fact, I've seen the records where you convinced her to list you as Winnie's guardian," he said.

I pursed my lips. Of course, Dylan Riggs dug around in my private matters. He was a former lawman, and future private investigator. Feeling no anger toward him, I said, "I think you have better options."

"Would you just stop? Jeremiah has always said you don't belong in a trailer park, and he's right. I don't know why you insist on staying here now that everyone knows who you are. You've taken on this huge responsibility. You've handled it like true royalty. I know that we've not made any future plans together, but you'd make a wonderful mother," he said.

"You would," Levi said from the door of the front bedroom. I hadn't heard him enter the room.

"You stay out of this, Levi Rearden," I said.

"Yes, ma'am," he said, plopping down on the couch.

"Grace, we don't have to talk about this now, but you need to

69

start seeing yourself differently. You've taken on responsibilities, and it has created something new in this world. A haven for exiles. You are a mother to all of us in a way. Protecting us, and spanking us when we get out of line," he grinned.

"You!" I said pointing a finger at him.

"Me, what?" The smile grew wider.

"Don't sweet talk me, Dylan Riggs," I protested.

"Two days, Grace," he said holding up two fingers as Levi laughed.

Two long days.

December 19th

DYLAN AND I LEFT EARLY THE NEXT MORNING TO STAKE OUT THE Food Mart in hopes of pre-empting the yogurt fiend. We sat in his cruiser eating biscuits that Luther packed up for us along with two cups of coffee from Nestor's bar.

"Sorry, if I pushed too hard last night," he said.

"I'm fine. I don't see myself that way, but you didn't make me mad," I admitted.

"Just uncomfortable," he said.

"Yes, some, but I don't want to see myself as any sort of hero or anything. I've done my fair share of fairy mischief over the years," I admitted.

"Like what?" he asked.

"You don't want to know," I replied.

"Sure, I do. You weren't cow tipping, were you?" he laughed.

"No, most of my mischief involved men," I said.

"Oh, you are right. I don't want to know," he said. I glanced toward him hoping to see if he was angry, but a playful light danced in his eye.

"You aren't innocent either," I said.

"Whatever. I am a bastion of virtue," he said.

I almost sprayed coffee all over his dash. He laughed. "I doubt that," I said.

"Why?" he asked.

"You are too damn good looking not to have women falling all over you for however many years you've been on this earth," I said.

"I was born in 1542. I became the phoenix when I was 18. There have been women, but none like you," he said.

"Flatterer! Damn, you are old!" I said.

"You are older than me, aren't you?" he asked.

"Yes," I muttered not giving him anything. I wasn't sure what year I was born because I was born in the Otherworld. Time wasn't the same there as it was here. I knew I started roaming with the gypsies in Europe in the late middle ages. He knew better than to ask. "Thank you."

"For?" he said while chewing on the last of his biscuit.

"Saying none of them were like me," I said.

He grinned. "It's the truth. You are my first fairy queen."

"Oh, just another notch on your belt," I teased.

"Yep. Damn fine notch," he replied, but his face changed quickly. "Grace, look at that woman."

I turned to see a woman dressed in tall black boots, black jeans and a long black duster. "Goth emo tweaker?" I asked.

"Look at her with your fairy eyes," he said.

Drawing on the power in my tattoo, it flared blue in the car illuminating the inside. I looked at the woman who seethed in a black smoky power. "What the hell?" I muttered. "Do you recognize her?"

Dylan, while the sheriff knew every person in the county, shook his head. "Witch."

"What?" I said staring at her through my normal sight.

"She's a witch," he said.

"How do you know?" I asked.

"We talk about the phoenix, but the thunderbird in me knows evil when it sees it," he said. "Don't draw attention over here. Call Levi and get him down here. You go home with him."

"No way. I'm not leaving you here," I said.

"I can handle her. Grace, if she's one of the coven, then she's here to make sure you die," he suggested.

"You think that is Lisette?" I asked. Levi had never described her to me, other than she looked exotic, which translated to fuckable in my fairy brain. This woman didn't have anything exotic about her. In fact, she looked like she was trying to hard to be gothy.

The woman had pale skin and deep expressive eyes. She paced on the sidewalk just outside the entrance to the grocery store. She was talking on a cell phone, gesturing with her right hand.

I picked up my phone to call Levi. If it was Lisette or any of her coven, he would know. It rang several times, and he answered breathing heavily.

"What?" he growled.

"There is a witch here at the Food Mart. Dylan thinks it might be one of the Cane Creek Coven. I need you to get down here," I said.

"Tell her to fuck off," I heard a female voice in the background.

"Oh, Levi, I'm sorry. Don't worry about it," I said hanging up the phone.

"Why did you do that!" Dylan yelled.

"He's fucking Kady at the moment. It's bad enough they are fighting because of me. I can't call him down here now!" I said. "I want him to be happy."

Dylan growled and dialed him back on his own phone. Before Levi even spoke, Dylan said, "Get your ass down here now!"

I heard Levi mumble something, and Dylan hung up on him.

"I wish you hadn't done that," I said.

"Look at me," he said. I turned to meet his eyes. "If they are here, they are here to kill you and take him. We have to know."

"I don't disagree, but poor Levi," I said.

"If she is that immature, he needs to get away from her," he said. If I looked at it that way, he was right. Kady seemed to flip flop, but I thought it to be pretty typical of the young women I knew. Ella Jenkins was the same way. She was the mayor's daughter and notorious in her sexual exploits. Of course, she was half-fairy like Levi. He wasn't interested in her.

We watched the woman as she spoke on the phone. "I'm going to talk to her. Just friendly like until Levi gets here. You stay in the car. Please, Grace."

"I will. I promise."

"You owe me so many minutes right now," he grinned as he got out of the car.

"We can negotiate the total in a couple days," I said smiling.

"Stay!" he said shutting the door.

I watched him grab a cart from the corral, pushing it toward the door. She hung up the phone as he approached. I wished I could hear their conversation, but it seemed like she was charmed by his smile and friendly manner. Turning to look at the main road, I waited to see if Levi had arrived yet. When I turned back around, the woman had latched on to Dylan's arm. He seemed more transfixed with her than the other way around.

I grabbed for the car handle to get out and pulled. It wouldn't open. I started jerking it as hard as I could. "Dylan!" I screamed.

She leered toward me struggling in the car as a knowing smile grew on her face. A green Camry pulled up to the curb. As she shoved Dylan into the back seat, she waved at me. Levi entered the lot driving my truck, stopping in the middle of the road. I slammed my fists on the window of the car. I didn't care if it broke and cut me. I had to stop them from taking Dylan.

Seeing his face through the window as they drove by, his eyes looked blank. The woman driving the car didn't look toward me because her eyes were fixed on Levi who stood in the middle of the road blocking her exit. The driver slammed on the gas as Levi jumped out of the way at the last second.

I started screaming at him. Running to me, he watched the direction of the vehicle as it turned out of the lot. He opened the door from the outside like it wasn't locked.

"Why didn't you stop them?" he asked.

As I bounded out of the car, I said, "I tried, you idiot. The door was locked by a spell."

"You couldn't have frozen it or something?" he yelled chasing me toward the truck.

"I don't know!" I said thinking I should probably consider spending time practicing battle magic. It seemed more and more these days I'd need it.

"Let me drive," he said, as I climbed into the truck. I slid across the seat, and he jumped into the cab with me. He tore out of the parking lot as I dialed Troy Maynard.

"Troy! A witch just kidnapped Dylan at the Food Mart," I said trying to catch my breath.

"When?" he said.

"Just now. Levi and I are chasing them down Hwy 114 south toward Mt. Hebron. We are losing them. Hurry up, Levi!" I shouted.

"I'll follow as quickly as I can. Be careful, Grace," Troy said as I heard the siren on his cruiser come to life.

Speeding down the two-lane state highway, I gripped the seat as Levi accelerated to catch the Camry. The car turned a curve as if it were on rails. Once we got to the curve, the car had disappeared, but there were no turn offs nearby.

"No!" I screamed slamming the dash.

Levi continued to follow the road, but we never saw them again.

"Which one was her?" I asked.

"The driver," he muttered. "I'm sorry, Grace." He pulled over to the side of the road as we waited for Troy to catch up.

Putting my hands on his cheeks, I said, "Honey, I don't blame you. How mad is Kady?"

"She's pissed," he muttered.

I wrapped my arms around him, crying into his neck. "I'm sorry, Dublin."

"We will get him back," he said. "Kady will get over it."

"Damn straight we will," I said. "We need to go back to his car. I need something to track him."

Troy pulled up next to us. Levi rolled down the window. "We lost them."

"Show me where you last saw them," he said.

We drove back up the road toward Shady Grove a couple of miles to the curve where we lost sight of the Camry. Getting out of the truck, we looked up and down the sides of the road for a hidden turn off.

Turning on my fairy sight, I looked and saw the faint residue of a spell, but I wasn't sure exactly what it was.

"You see it?" I asked Levi.

"Yes, but I don't know what it is. Concealment, maybe," he said.

"Where?" Troy asked.

I indicated the general area. Troy turned circles in the spot breathing deeply. "Smells like swamp," he said.

"Bayou priestesses," I offered.

"You guys, go back to town. I'm going to shift and track the scent. It's easier to track in wolf form. Make sure there aren't any others in town," he said.

"I don't want to leave him out here," I protested.

"I'll call you as soon as I have something," Troy said.

"I'd rather stay here if it's all the same to you," I said.

"Okay, just stay by the truck. Better yet inside it. Don't let them take you, Grace. He'd kill me if I let something happen to you," Troy said. "If they are after you or Levi, they will offer Dylan back to us."

"No, he won't kill you. You fall under my protection just like everyone else," I said. "Even from Dylan Riggs."

"I'll find him," he said as he took a wide stance in the center of the state highway. Exploding into fur, he turned into an ebony wolf. He sniffed the ground as he spun in the spot where the spell residual hovered over the road. He whined looking at me, but then took off south. He was fast. Faster than a normal canine. His form blurred away down the road leaving Levi and I standing at the truck.

"Get in, Grace," Levi said. "Just in case we have to move quickly."

"Okay," I muttered as he helped me into the truck.

My phone rang. "Hello," I answered.

"Grace, why is Dylan's car sitting in the parking lot of the Food Mart with the door open?" Nestor asked.

"The swamp witches are in town. They took him," I muttered as tears rolled down my cheek.

"Give me," Levi said, reaching for the phone. He took it from me and explained to Nestor what happened. "Don't worry. I've got her."

Levi hung up the phone handing it back to me. I leaned my head back, staring at the ceiling. "If I'd just died, maybe they wouldn't have come up here," I said. "We need to go back and get something of his."

"We will when Troy gets back," he said. "All of this goes back to my mistake, Grace."

"Don't do that right now, Dublin. Or I'll smack you," I said.

"I deserve to be smacked for being so stupid," he said. "We should call Jeremiah and tell him she's up here."

I handed him the phone back. He dialed Jeremiah, but it went straight to voice mail. "Jeremiah, get back to Shady Grove. Lisette and at least one other of the coven are in town. They took Dylan. We need your help."

He stuck the phone in his pocket, wrapping me up in his arms. I leaned into his chest as we waited.

"Fucking trolls. Fucking witches. What's next?" I blurted out.

"Don't ask that question. You might regret the answer," he said.

"You are probably right," I said. My cell phone rang in his pocket. "Fuck me."

"Okay," he said with a twinkle in his eye. I punched him in the shoulder as my phone rang. He answered. "Grace's phone."

"You have got to be kidding me?" Levi said, listening to the voice on the other end. It was definitely female. "I'll ask her what she wants to do, but we have a situation here, too."

"What?" I whispered.

He placed his hand over the phone. "Troll number eight has appeared. Troy is out here chasing the witches. Dylan is gone. They need someone to help," he grimaced.

"We will go. I can get something out of Dylan's car to track him while we are there. Where is the bastard?" I asked.

"At Sally's SnoCone Shack," he replied.

"Okay," I muttered.

"We are on the way, Mable," he said, cranking up the truck.

The Food Mart was the center store in a long strip mall. The Grove Diner sat in the front of the parking lot. As we approached, the patrons of the diner stood outside looking towards the grocery. Nestor's bar was on the same block, but not in the same parking lot as the strip mall. On the far-right end of the mall just past the nail salon, a small storage building sat with two windows. A small wooden porch was built across the front, and the hand painted sign proclaimed it to be Sally's SnoCone Shack. On top of the shack, a gangly fellow sat with his legs hanging off the roof. Sally stood with Mable at the entrance of the Food Mart looking terrified.

Levi pulled right up in front of the shack. As we got out the "brother" spoke, "My queen and her bard have come to sing for me!"

"Get down," I ordered him.

"Well, I'm afraid of heights, my Queen. It seems I cannot get down," he laughed.

Mable approached us cautiously. "He was ranting about Sally not having frozen custard. You know she only sells that during the summer," she said.

"I will bring you down if I have to," I said.

"Dearest Gloriana, you would do no harm to me. The view is nice up here," he chuckled swinging his legs.

"What do you want?" I attempted to negotiate.

"Some of Miss Sally's famous frozen custard. I've heard it tastes just like frozen skyr," he explained. "I've not had any skyr since I left the old country."

"I'm going to send your ass back to the old country. Get down now!" I screamed. I'd lost my patience. Dylan was more important than this nonsense.

"Come and get me," he teased. "I bet your custard is frozen too!"

"You son of a bitch," Levi growled.

"Hey! You know my mother!" he laughed swinging his legs.

I growled, "Fine!" Pushing power through my tattoo, I pointed my hand to the ground. The pavement turned to ice as Mable retreated to the safety of the grocery dragging Sally with her. A large cloud covered the sun, and the chilly temperatures dropped to frigid depths.

"Grace," Levi muttered.

"Shut up, Levi," I spouted at him. I twirled my hand in front of me creating a vortex of snow and wind. Stepping into it, my body thrust upward toward the troll.

"Agh! Help me! Help me! She's gone mad!" he squealed backing away from me.

Grabbing his shirt, I turned to throw him off the building as Levi begged me not to hurt him. So, I slung him at Levi who broke the troll's fall. They both skittered across the ice in a tangled web of flailing limbs.

"Get off me," Levi hissed shoving the troll off of him.

Allowing the wind to die down, I waved at the cloud, and the sun appeared again. As I stepped across the icy parking lot with ease, the snow ceased. "Take me to the jail with my brothers," he begged.

"No, I'm tired of this bullshit!" I railed. "You and your damn brothers are a menace. I am going to kill every single one of you!" I stood over him as he cowered covering his head.

Feeling my bard stalking behind me, I spun around on him. "Don't you fucking touch me or say a word," I said.

"There you are with her, again," a voice came from the grocery store exit. Kady stood with her hands on her hips staring at Levi.

"Listen here, Cunt. I am the only one that gets to berate my bard. You got that? Shut the fuck up. This doesn't concern you," I turned on her. Her eyes flashed with fear.

"Grace, I know you are upset, but you've got to calm down," Levi coaxed. "Please, don't let her take over."

"She is me! I am her! That's what all of you can't understand. The thing that keeps the bad guys away from Shady Grove is this! Me! The dreaded fairy Queen! You all wanted me to do this, but you had no idea what I'm actually capable of doing," I twirled talking to the patrons outside the diner who stood with Betty and Luther. "You provoke me. This is what you get!"

Turning back to Levi, his blue eyes watered on the edges. He dropped his head and slid across the lot to Kady dragging her back into the grocery. The diners returned to the safety of the diner. Mable stood inside the Food Mart staring at me, but I realized her mouth was moving. Was she casting a spell? Looking at her hand, her cell phone glowed with life.

"Gloriana, stand down," a thick deep voice came from behind me. Slowly I turned to see the black cloaked form of Caiaphas, the head of the Sanhedrin. His eyebrows were still overly bushy.

"No, this is my town. You don't get to control me anymore," I said as the troll tried to move away. "Stay still, varmint."

"You cannot display power like this. It's against your contract," he said.

"You can take my contract and shove it up your tight ass," I sneered.

He chuckled. "So belligerent. It's almost endearing."

"Your operative has failed to control the Cane Creek Coven. They are here and have taken Dylan Riggs. Forgive me if I'm a little testy!" I said.

"As you said, this is your town. Deal with it. Have fun, dear," he said fading away.

"Self-righteous, smug, mother fucker!" I screamed at the last remnant of his visage.

Trying to back down off the power coursing through my veins, my hands started to shake. I couldn't lose control. If I let it back off too much, I would die. The troll watched me as if I were about to implode. To be honest, it felt like I was.

"What's your name?" I asked him as my voice shook.

"Kevin," he muttered.

"I don't have time for you, Kevin. If you don't want to be bloody ice chunks of troll, I suggest you get off your ass and get into the bed of my truck," I said through clenched teeth.

He slipped while trying to stand up, but hurried over to the truck climbing in. The automatic doors of the grocery whooshed open, and Levi walked toward me.

"If you leave me now, we are done Levi Rearden!" Kady called behind him.

"Just stay with her," I muttered knowing he could hear me.

"Glad to see you've come to your senses," he said. "She will get over it. If she doesn't, oh well." Grabbing my arm, he led me to the truck. I climbed into the passenger side watching Kady scowl from the inside of the store. She really looked ugly at that moment. I always considered her very pretty, but as she punished Levi for his connection to me, I thought the troll in my truck looked way better than her.

He jumped in starting the truck up. We rode in silence to the holding cells for the Sheriff's department. I shook my hands along the way releasing the power little by little. Levi watched me closely as I did it.

When we arrived he said, "Stay here. I'll take him in."

He dragged Kevin off to holding to share a cell with his brothers. I waited in the truck, and my icy demeanor melted into tears. I buried my face in my hands. What a bitch. "I'll have to apologize to the whole town," I muttered to myself.

"A tad out of control, huh?" a deep voice said from the driver's seat. I jumped back, but quickly realized that my father had decided to visit.

"Daddy, what are you doing here?" I asked.

"When people get scared, they call the biggest bad guy to take care of the little one. Mable is a faithful servant. Although, if we were really to fight, I'm not so sure you wouldn't destroy me," he said plainly.

"Don't flatter me," I said.

"Gloriana, you are in uncharted territory. You are cursed. Your bard has serious baggage. Your, um, Dylan, what is he exactly? Pet? Boyfriend? Lover?" he stopped mid-thought.

"Daddy," I growled.

"Yes, well, Dylan is your foil and currently kidnapped. The trolls are amusing," he said chuckling.

"Get to the point, Daddy," I spouted at him.

"You've taken on responsibilities that I honestly never thought you ever would. With that power and responsibility comes trouble. It's just the way it is. A ruler must control their realm in the good times and in chaos. You just happen to be in the center of chaos. I know my advice is the last thing that you want, but I've come here to say this. You cannot control chaos, but it most certainly can control you. You cannot allow that to happen. Use the chaos to cement your leadership here. Rise above it. I know that you can," he said.

"I wasn't ready for this job," I said.

"You've been ready for this job since you were a child. It's in your blood. I know this, because it's my blood," he said smugly.

"Arrogant much?" I asked.

"There is a fine line between arrogance and confidence. Arrogance is confidence pushed down people's throats. Confidence is a beacon that they all want to follow, emulating your example. Your council idea is the right direction to take, but you must navigate the chaos to get there," he said. "I know you can do it."

"Thank you, Daddy," I whispered.

"You are welcome, my beautiful child," he said fading away.

My tears continued because I didn't have the same confidence that he had in me. Levi walked out of the building as Sheriff Maynard pulled into the lot.

Jumping out of the truck, I ran to where he parked his cruiser. "I heard you caught a troll," he said.

"Yes, he's inside," Levi said.

"I found him," Troy said.

"Where is he?" I gasped.

"They are in the old Palmer place on Milltown Road. The scent ran up to the house, but I didn't get close enough to set off any traps. Let me grab some back-up, and we will go after him," he said, heading toward the building.

"Was that your father?" Levi asked me.

"Yes," I said. "You saw him?"

"I came out before and you didn't see me. I ducked back into the building to let him talk to you," he said.

"He has far more faith in my abilities than I deserve," I muttered. "I'm sorry about Kady."

"Grace, Kady knows that we aren't doing anything. She's making excuses to get out of our relationship. I haven't figured out why yet, but it doesn't matter. The town is a mad house, and you need me," he said.

"I do need you, Troy, and everyone else," I said hugging him.

"I'm telling Dylan," Troy grinned from the steps at the doorway with his girlfriend Amanda Capps standing next to him. Amanda and I didn't get along, but she was a wolf, too. Her help would be better than any of the vanilla human deputies in the force. She'd joined the department on the lowest level, working her way back up the ranks after her mistakes with my lawyer, Lysander. Troy made sure that other officers approved her work schedules and assignments. No one questioned his relationship with her.

I watched her closely as well, in case she decided to dabble in the darkness again. For the most part, she was a dedicated mother. She and Troy were working on mending the broken pieces of the relationship they'd had, but both lone wolves found a natural connection to each other. I watched, keeping my distance.

"We gotta get him back before you can tattle," I said.

"We will," he said.

"Yes, we will," Levi said.

"What are we waiting on?" I asked.

"What's the plan?" I asked Troy as we crouched in the forest. The night blanketed over us, and the stars flickered in the cold night. The moon, almost full, illuminated the ground around us.

"Amanda and I will circle around the back. When Levi starts to play, you need to cast a spell to trigger the traps so we can see them. Once the traps are neutralized, we move in," he said.

"Let me handle them. If possible, you get Dylan out, and leave them to me. That is, if for some reason they aren't incapacitated by Levi," I said. They both nodded, stalking away, then bursting into fur. They took a circular route to the back of the dilapidated house. Dylan and I had been here before together. The house was abandoned, but we found a moonshine still. The moonshine burned our throats, but it was effective. Dylan was pissed that I had dared him to drink it, but he quickly got over it. I smiled thinking about the adventure prior to our first tryst.

"You okay?" Levi asked.

"Yes, just memories," I said.

"Good ones, apparently," he said.

"I love him," I said.

"You should probably tell him that," he scolded.

"Well then, you better play your heart out, Dublin," I said.

"Yes, ma'am," he said as he strapped on the guitar stepping into the moonlit grass in front of the house. His fingers glided along the strings. Usually, we employed the lullaby technique for putting our victims to sleep. I suspected that the witches would anticipate that move, so I decided on something more, Gracesque. The melody resembled a power love ballad from an eighties hair band. He slowly approached the front door of the house. Through the windows, I could see movement as the occupants responded to his song.

Gripping the oak tree that I'd positioned myself against, I drew power then forced a cold wind along the grass at breakneck speed. Several audible pops resounded around the house.

"Keep playing, baby," I encouraged him from behind. His fingers deftly flowed over the strings. The combination of the movement of his hands and the power of the music was mesmerizing.

I stalked behind him to avoid the brunt of the spell as he continued the fiery ballad. It was the kind that made girls throw their panties at the guitarist at a concert. Hell, I wanted to throw my panties at him. We weren't sure if the song would affect the wolves, but I suspected if they were shifted before it started, they wouldn't be.

Levi's foot touched the first step leading to the wooden porch. The door slowly opened and a caramel skinned woman with dark locks sashayed out to him. Once he reached the top step, she ran her claws across his chest, and he shivered.

"Keep playing, Levi," I urged him forward. Once inside the first room of the house, another woman stalked down the stairs to him. Her skin, pale as the moon, glistened with sweat. She locked arms with the other woman as they began kissing each other.

"Oh, shit," Levi murmured.

I tried not to giggle. "Stay on target," I muttered.

"Copy, Gold Five," he returned.

"Huh?"

"Never mind," he said as he continued to play. "Which way?"

I paused looking up the stairs. Out of the corner of my eye, I saw a fur ball dart around the corner in the kitchen. I nodded toward the kitchen. As we turned into the room being followed by the nympho witches, another woman approached Levi. Her eyes were almost completely black. Dark black hair cascaded down past her shoulders. Her hips shifted back and forth as she approached him. It was the goth girl that took Dylan. He gulped.

"Keep it together, Stud," I said as she rubbed body up and down his side. She planted her lips on his neck, and the song faulted. "Levi!"

He picked back up the song as I wedged myself between her and him. "Sorry, no autographs until after the show," I told her. She pouted, but continued to sway to the music following us into the dining room. The other two witches pulled her into their grasp, then the twosome became a threesome. The wolves stood on each side of the table. Dylan laid on the table moaning as the coven leader, Lisette writhed astride him.

"Well, damn it," I said rushing toward her. Encasing my fist in ice, I struck her across the jaw. Her body flew across the room, slamming against the far wall. She slid down the wall unconscious. Daring to look at his crotch, I sighed realizing she was only dry humping him. The wolves whined. Dylan raised up from the table, looked at Levi, then locked eyes with me.

"Dylan, honey, are you okay?"

Succumbing to the enthrallment, he slid off the table, so I

backed away not wanting him to touch me. "Dylan, wake up. Levi stop playing."

"What about the witches?" he asked as his fingers continued on autopilot.

"He can't touch me!" I exclaimed.

Levi's song intensified in his indecision. Dylan turned his eyes from me to Levi. Dylan grabbed him by the shirt locking lips with him. Levi immediately stopped playing and tried pushing him away. "Oh, god, no!" he gagged.

Dylan's eyes fluttered after the song stopped, realizing he had embraced Levi. I covered my mouth suppressing a laugh. "What the hell?" he shoved Levi away. He spun around to me and the wolves, who snorted.

"Dylan, man, I like you, but you aren't my type," Levi said red-faced.

Dylan was so confused twisting back and forth when the three witches from the kitchen awakened from the enthrallment and started chanting. My eyes twitched to Lisette still passed out on the floor. "We gotta go now," I said as I picked a dusty chair from the table, smashing it against the dining room window. The wolves jumped through.

I turned back to the witches who approached with hands raised. Their pupils widening across their eyes. Forcing power through my tattoo, I built a flimsy ice wall between us.

"Come on, Dylan," Levi said, grabbing his arm.

"Don't fucking touch me," Dylan scowled.

"Go through the window, Dylan!" I screamed.

Levi tossed his guitar out the window, jumping out behind it. Dylan still looked puzzled. "Darlin', it's time to go," I said. He blinked at me using the name he had requested and grinned.

"Well, what are you waiting on?" he laughed.

"You! Go!" I ordered as he jumped out the window. I followed close behind hearing the ice wall breaking. We ran in the darkness toward where we had parked the vehicles.

9

December 20th

Breathing hard, I leaned against the truck smirking at Dylan and Levi, who wouldn't look at each other. Troy and Amanda had returned to human form, putting on clothes they'd stowed in the sheriff's cruiser.

The moon had started to sink into the west, and a cool stillness enveloped us.

"So?" I said.

"Don't even say anything, Grace," Dylan growled. I giggled, and I heard Amanda behind me trying not to laugh.

"It was a spell," I said.

"I know what it was," he spouted.

"Sorry," Levi muttered. I almost lost it, but bit my lip to spare myself the wrath of Mr. Sandy Hair. However, the demon inside of me won.

"Now we've both kissed him," I said. Troy and Amanda died laughing. Dylan's smile quirked on the edge of his mouth.

"You are better than he is," Levi said.

"Shut up!" Dylan said, but started to laugh. He stalked toward me trapping me with his arms against the truck. "I still can't touch you."

"Not until midnight," I said.

"It's past midnight," he said.

"Midnight tonight," I frowned. The tension between us was like sparks of lighting. My memories drifted back to the night he kissed me in the street after the pool game at the bar. He kept his body from touching me then, refusing to give into his desires. This tension was worse because it wasn't by choice.

"I'm going to ride back with Troy," Levi said interrupting us.

"Okay, honey. You did great," I said.

"Hey Dylan, you need some lip moisturizer, Dude," he teased rubbing one of his fingers over his own lips.

"If you don't get in that damn car, Levi, I'm going to knock your lights out," he growled. Levi laughed.

He turned his attention back to me. "You said it," he laughed.

"Something had to jar you from the euphoria after kissing Levi. Trust me. I understand, because the kid knows how to kiss," I smirked hoping he would finally see the humor in it. He did as his eyes lit up. The moon reflected in them making them look icy. "Are you okay? She spelled the car door, and I couldn't get out."

"I saw everything happening, but couldn't do anything to stop it. I hate feeling helpless," he said. "In there, she was on me as soon as the music started, then I was out of it, too." I desperately wanted to touch him. Searching within myself, I wondered if I could hold back the curse and comfort him if just only for a moment.

Pushing power through my tattoo, my hand frosted over as I reached up to his cheek. He started to pull away, but with my empty hand, I grasped his shirt. I touched his cheek, and he groaned. I felt the frost melting, so I pushed harder knowing that it might make me woozy. It didn't matter because I was touching him.

"Grace, if you faint here, I can't pick you up," he said softly leaning into my fingertips.

I pulled away with no dizziness at all. "I'm glad you are okay. We dragged Levi out of bed with Kady. She broke up with him, again. I needed to know if it was Lisette. You missed the latest brother."

"Oh, really?" he said stepping back from me slipping his hands into his jean pockets. "Get in the truck and tell me about it on the way home."

As we drove back to Shady Grove, I told him about the troll on the shack. Not holding back, I told him about losing it at the Food Mart and the visit from my father.

"If I didn't know better, I'd think he actually loved you," he said as we pulled into my spot in front of the trailer. The icicle lights that Levi hung for me glittered in the darkness, and I could see the Christmas tree through the window lit up.

"Maybe. Or he doesn't want me to make a fool of him," I said.

"I'm proud of you. Did that sound condescending?" he asked.

"Yes, but I appreciate it just the same," I smiled.

We went inside to find Levi sitting on the couch talking on the cell phone. I grabbed a couple of sodas out of the fridge, giving him a sad look as Dylan and I ducked into my room. He pointed at Dylan who'd already turned his back.

"Psst, Dylan," I said getting him to turn and look at Levi.

"Huh?" he said.

Levi Rearden flashed a grin and winked at him. I clamped my hand over my mouth as Dylan slammed the door out of my hand. "He's going to torture you now," I said.

"If I were gay, Levi isn't my type," he said.

"Oh really? What's your type?" I asked.

"Little nerdy guys with glasses," he teased.

"He's been playing fantasy card games with the nerd crew from church," I offered. "He might know someone."

"I knew he was a nerd at heart," he teased.

I laughed more as I popped the top on the orange soda, sucking it down. He opened and drank his as well, while staring at me.

"You staying?" I asked.

"Yes. How are you feeling?" he asked.

"Tired, but I'm afraid if I go to sleep I'll lose my grip," I said.

"You lay down and rest. I'll watch out for you," he said.

I didn't know how he'd do that, but I trusted him with my life.

My heart. My everything. Dylan Riggs had successfully turned me into a sap.

I slept until morning. When I woke up, he'd moved one of the dining room chairs into the room, watching me with brilliant blue eyes.

"Morning, Sunshine," he said.

"Morning," I grumped pulling the covers over my head.

"Time to get up and meet the next brother," he said.

"What? Already?" I said.

"No, but you know it's coming," he said. "Can I take you to lunch?"

"Sure. What time is it?" I asked.

"Eleven," he said.

"Oh, shit! Why didn't you wake me up? Did you sleep?" I asked.

"Yes, I slept. I let Levi watch you for a few hours, and you needed the rest. You looked terrible," he said.

I threw a pillow at him. "Ass," I said.

"I have a nice ass," he said.

"Yes, you do," I mumbled climbing out of the bed. "I'll get a shower and get ready."

"Okay. Levi left earlier. I think he was going to meet Kady at the bar so they could talk over coffee," he said.

"Smart move on his part. The coffee," I said.

"He's learning," he said.

"Now if I could keep the two of you apart," I teased.

"You, Grace. I only want you," he said.

"I know," I replied.

"You know, huh?" he laughed.

"Yep," I said ducking into the bathroom.

I heard him sigh on the other side of the door. Soon, darlin', soon.

"I thought we were going to the diner," I said.

He pulled into Brad's Smokehouse BBQ which was just south of town. "No, I promised Brad that I'd come by and try his new pulled pork. He's trying out a new rub."

"Rub?" I asked.

"It's the seasoning he puts on the pork before he smokes it," he explained.

"Hm. Not nearly as kinky as I hoped," I said.

He laughed. "Not nearly."

I wore my own clothes today. Jeans and a slouchy sweater. The curse was weighing on me, so I didn't generate my own clothes with my power. I was using everything I had to stay alive. However, the last thing I wanted Dylan to know was how close I was to losing it. Just a few more hours and I could go back to being myself. Most of all, I wanted his lips on mine. Oh, hell, I wanted his everything on my everything.

He held the door open for me as we went into the cabin-like restaurant.

"Hey, Riggs!" Brad called from the back. He came around the counter wearing a white apron without a spot on it. He was a curious fellow with slender legs, more than just a little belly and a large head that looked a tad too big for his body. However, he was extremely nice and would talk your ear off if you let him.

"Hey Brad!" Dylan said clasping hands with him. Bro handshake.

"Y'all come in and sit. Oh, man, the pork is good today," he said. "I'll bring you out a little of everything." He didn't look at me or say a word to me.

"I think he ignored me," I said as we sat down at the table.

"You probably intimidate him," he said.

"I don't know him," I said. I only had a passing knowledge of the local BBQ guru. He competed in BBQ competitions across the country, and the trophies were displayed all around the room.

He shook his head. "Grace, in this form, you could drive any man over the edge."

"But you prefer the other," I said.

"Yes," he said.

"Why?" I asked.

"I just prefer brunettes," he said.

"That's it?" I asked.

"Yep, that's it," he returned. I shrugged.

Brad brought out a plate of something fried and set it down on the table.

"What's that?" I asked.

He didn't respond.

"Riggs, man, you gotta try these fried pickles," he said as the waitress set two glasses of soda down on the table. I knew her from church.

"Hey Tonya," I said. She flashed a smile at me. Her dark red hair was bundled-up behind her head in a ponytail that swished back and forth as she walked. She was a beauty. She was a siren.

"Grace, it's good to see you. You are looking awfully blonde," she commented.

"Curse," I said.

"Damn, that sucks," she replied. "If y'all need anything, just let me know."

"Thanks girl," I said as she trotted away. Brad watched her swaying ponytail as she left. Dylan liked brunettes. Brad liked gingers. I wondered what Levi liked. Kady had brown hair, but it was much lighter than mine as Grace.

"Brad, bring out some of that sausage I had last time," Dylan said.

"Yeah, man, sure thing. I'll fix you up," he said disappearing into the kitchen.

Our lunch date reminded me of the lunches that we used to have before we slept together. We spent very little time talking about business. Focusing on trivial things like football teams and television shows, Dylan and I enjoyed each other's company. Back then, I didn't even bother making a move on him, because of his live-in girlfriend, Stephanie. I'd since learned that she cheated on him from day one, but apparently, he knew. Either he didn't care, or it didn't bother him. When she left, or rather he kicked her out, he turned to me. I was more than happy to oblige him for the one-night stand. I never imagined my heart would get wrapped up into it.

"What are you thinking about?" he asked leaning back in his chair poking his belly out as if he had a pot belly like St. Nick. Dylan didn't have a fat bone on his body. I'd seen it. All of it. Sigh.

"About our old lunches," I said.

"Yeah? What about them?" he asked.

"You called them business lunches," I said.

He wrinkled his nose. "What are you getting at, Grace?"

"You were with her all that time. Why go to lunch with me?"

"Stephanie and I had a complicated relationship. I know that sounds like a status on a dating site, but looking back, we were more roommates than lovers. I'll be honest with you. We had our romps, but as time went by the romps got less and less. It was more just a convenience. A date when there was a function. A warm body in the bed at night. I know now that it wasn't love," he said.

"I'm sorry. I didn't mean to pry. Just thinking more about us," I said.

"You can ask me whatever you want. Whatever you need, Grace," he said leaning forward on the table.

"You've been on this earth a long time. I suppose there has been more than one Stephanie," I said.

"Actually no. Grace, part of the reason I understand you so well, is that I know how you operate. Or at least, how you used to operate. A long, long string of one-nighters. No attachments," he said.

I looked down at my hands as I fidgeted with my fingers. "Why did you stay with her? I mean, why did you decide to stop the flings?"

"When I heard about Shady Grove, something inside of me ached to just stay in one place. To find happiness. I thought she was it," he said.

I smiled, because I knew he thought I was it. Two months ago, that would have made me pack my bags and run to a trailer park far, far away. Now, when I couldn't touch him at all, I wanted him more than ever.

"Hey, look at me," he said. Lifting my head to his brilliant blue eyes, I smiled to match his. "We are almost there. Just a few more hours. There is a party tonight, right?"

"Yes, the tree lighting, food and drinks in the plaza. I think the kids from the elementary school will be doing a pageant and singing," I said.

"Will you be my date?" he asked.

"Who else would I go with?" I asked. "But I understand if you would rather go with Levi."

His eyes twinkled despite my jab at his unfortunate kiss with Levi. "You are supposed to say yes, Grace."

"Yes, Grace," I said as he glared at me. "I will be your date. Fat lot of good it will do us. I can't touch you!"

"I'll wear my leather jacket, and you wear some gloves or something," he suggested.

"You are warm all over, Darlin'. Doesn't matter what I wear or you wear to block it," I said.

His hand rested on the edge of the table. His index finger lightly tapping. He saw me staring at it, longing to touch it. "Okay, let's go before we both go nuts."

"I'm already gone," I said.

"Well, I didn't want to mention it. I figured that was a sure-fired way to not get laid," he said.

"How crude," I gasped.

"Oh please, little Miss Potty Mouth," he said as he left money on the table for the bill.

I grimaced a little because I had been trying to clean up my language. It wasn't proper for the queen to walk around spouting profanities. However, I was finding it extremely difficult. Walking outside he watched me contemplate. I looked up to meet his eyes.

"What?"

"You done?" he asked.

"Done what?"

"Brooding," he said. "I swear you've been around Levi too much."

"That should turn you on," I laughed making a kissy face.

Digging through all the drawers in my dresser and throwing clothes all over the bed, I had yet to find the right thing to wear to the plaza that evening.

Levi darkened my bedroom doorway, surveying the damage.

"I swear, Grace, you have more clothes than any woman I've ever known. How do you get all of that in your closet?" he smirked.

"Magic," I muttered as I continued to dig.

"What are you looking for?" he asked.

"Something that doesn't make me look like a whore," I replied. "All of these look like they came from strippersrus.com!"

He chuckled. "Just wear some jeans and a sweater like you did earlier today. What's the big deal?"

"You know what the big deal is, Levi Rearden. Don't make me slap you," I said.

"I might let you depending on where you place the slap," he said.

"I could never come between you and Dylan," I smirked back at him.

He smiled, "No one could steal that man's heart from you. No matter how the sparks flew between us, I knew he was yours."

I died laughing. "You are crazy, Dublin. So, Kady?"

"No, actually I'm taking Ella tonight," he said.

"What? Really?" I was shocked. He met Ella one of his first days in Shady Grove. He clearly found her attractive, but said she wasn't his type. I supposed he meant whore fairy, but that had never stopped him from admiring me.

"I thought I'd give it a chance. She calls me all the time," he boasted.

"Liar!"

"Okay, well, she did call me today and asked me to go with her," he said.

"So, you said yes?" I asked.

"Kadence is so done with me," he muttered. "At least, I can go and have fun. I hear Ella is a sure thing."

Walking up to him, I embraced him feeling the tingle between us. "I love ya, Levi. Don't do anything you'll regret. I mean, you are gorgeous even when you are brooding, but you are tender hearted. Don't break your own heart in the process of trying to fill it."

"Damn, when did you become so poignant?" he said as he hugged me back.

"Since I did a fool thing, by falling in love," I said.

He pulled back and looked at me. "You haven't told him yet?"

"He knows," I said.

"Doesn't matter. You still have to say it. Do it tonight. Don't wait any longer, Grace," he suggested.

"I won't. I promise," I said.

"Now get dressed, I'm leaving in thirty minutes," he turned, slapping me on the ass.

My face turned fifty shades of red, and I charged him. He ran through the trailer squealing like a pig. "Levi Rearden! You are going to get it!" He beat me to his bedroom. The door slammed in my face as I heard him laughing on the other side. "Twenty-nine minutes!"

"Damn it!" I said skulking back to my room.

Twenty minutes passed as I sat on my bed looking at the carnage of clothes lying around my bed. Levi appeared at the door again with a long, wrapped box. He chucked it over to the bed, and it landed next to me.

"It's not Christmas," I said.

"Open the damn box and get dressed. Dylan called. He's on his way," he said.

"Shit!" I said. Picking up the box, my eyes watered a little. Pulling off the paper, I looked up to him. He wore a cheesy grin that made me want it kiss him. In a purely platonic way, of course. Opening the box and folding the paper back, I found a deep plum sweater. I pulled it out of the box, touching the soft sleeves. It would hang off one shoulder the way the neck was cut.

"Do you like it?" he asked timidly.

"It's lovely. Did she pick it out?" I asked.

"No, a couple of days ago I rode into town with Nestor to pick up his coffee supply. He let me out at the mall. I liked the color," he said.

Jumping off the bed, I hugged him tightly for the second time that afternoon. "Thank you, Levi," I said.

"I'm glad you like it. Now, get on some skinny jeans and boots. Hurry up!" he said pushing me away.

Piecing my outfit together with his suggestions, I stared at myself in the mirror. It was the right kind of sexy and nice. More Grace than Gloriana. However, even looking at my platinum locks and turquoise eyes in the mirror, I realized that I looked different. Even to myself. My soul had changed. My heart had changed. It was written in the depths of my eyes.

As I admired myself in the mirror, Mr. Sandy Hair stepped into the reflection. "Wow," he said grinning. He walked up behind me. Standing as close as he could without touching, I heard him breathe in deeply.

He wore dark jeans with a tan Henley sweater and my favorite leather jacket. His scent enveloped me. His hair, which had grown longer on the top, was tousled perfectly. I gawked at him. "You look fantastic," I said.

He stared at my bare shoulder cutting his eyes to me in the mirror. He leaned forward like he was going to take a bite. My heart pounded because I wanted him to do it. At the last moment, I spun around. "I wasn't going to do it," he teased. "At least not yet. You ready?"

"In more ways than one," I admitted.

"Come on," he nodded toward the door.

We parked just down the road from the plaza and walked close to each other. The tree was towered above the center of the small park across from city hall. The streets were blocked off as children ran freely. Vendors had all sorts of foods and crafts. I saw BBQ Brad set up with a small cart near the edge of the park. He waved to Dylan as we approached.

"Man, I'm glad you didn't eat all my sausage today," he said. "It's selling like crazy out here."

"Brad, I told you that it's the best smoked sausage I've ever had," Dylan told him.

"Yeah, I know, man. But I just didn't realize. I'm so busy. Talk to ya later, man," Brad said taking money from the hands of starving townspeople.

Dylan and I walked around the plaza greeting everyone that we knew. Thankfully no one called me "Queen."

Large strings of Christmas lights hung between the light fixtures in the plaza surrounding the large unlit Christmas tree. The center gazebo was lined with lights and illuminated the area with night quickly approaching.

Hearing a shriek behind me, I turned to catch Winnie as she barreled into my arms, dressed as an angel complete with a tinsel halo. "Aunt Grace, look at me! I'm an angel," she said, jumping out of my arms and twirling.

"You look fantastic, Winnie! I can't wait to see your program," I said.

"Hey, Mr. Dylan," she said to him shyly. Normally she high-fived him or tried to punch him playfully.

"Hello, Winnie. You look beautiful," he said.

Her cheeks flushed pink. The kid had a crush on him. I couldn't blame her. "I'm going to have to hide you from Winnie," I said as she ran off to meet her friends.

"She's a catch. I don't know how I'll choose," he said.

Night quickly fell as we all gathered around the darkened tree. I saw Levi arm in arm with Ella Jenkins across the way. He smiled as she chattered on. I didn't see Kady at all. Or her father Bro. Matthew Rayburn.

The children lined up in front of the tree as the Mayor stood on a small wooden platform with a microphone. "Good evening, Shady Grove!" he called to the crowd. They all responded cheerfully.

"I welcome you all this evening to the annual tree lighting ceremony. Let's get to it! I'll start the countdown. 5…4…3…2…1!" he shouted as the town counted with him.

As the tree erupted with lights, the crowd cheered.

"Alright now. Let's listen to these angels sing!" he said indicating the children all dressed in white robes with tinsel halos.

They sang "O Christmas Tree" and "We Wish You a Merry Christmas" to the pleasure of all those who listened. They finished with a sweet rendition of "The First Noel." The crowd clapped as the children dispersed running to their parents as the night grew colder and darker. Winnie stood there confused. I looked around and didn't see Bethany.

"I got her," Dylan said. He walked up to her bending down to her level. Her bottom lip quivered, and he scooped her up in his arms bringing her over to me.

"Mommy isn't here," she whimpered.

"How did you get here?" I asked.

"Pastor Zeke from my church picked me up, but mommy said she was coming," she pouted.

"I'm sure she wanted to be here," I said.

"No, she never wants to see me sing," she said.

"I thought you were magnificent," I said moving her thoughts from her mother.

"Me, too," Dylan added.

Levi strode over with Ella on his arm. "Winnie, you did so good!"

"Uncle Levi!" she squealed lunging toward him. He took her in his arms as Ella backed off with a scowl. I locked eyes with her, and she faked a smile towards the adoring Winnie.

"She needs a coat," Levi said.

"Winnie, did you wear a coat?" I asked.

"No, ma'am. My old one didn't fit," she said.

"Here use this," a familiar female voice said from behind us.

We all turned to see Kadence Rayburn and her father standing there. She offered her blanket scarf. "Thank you, Kady," I said turning to Dylan wide-eyed. "We will get you a new coat tomorrow, Winnie. Want to go shopping?" I chattered to avoid the tension in the air.

"This is soft. Thank you, Kady," Winnie said.

"You are welcome, sweetheart," she said. "Grace, that is a lovely sweater."

"Thanks. It was an early Christmas present," I said without mentioning Levi who stood frozen with Winnie in his arms, Ella by his side, and Kady giving him the stink-eye.

"Well, how about we take Winnie home?" Dylan said.

"No, I want to stay with Uncle Levi," she said clinging to his neck.

He smiled and patted her on the back. "I'll take you home," he said. "You need your sleep for shopping tomorrow."

"Can we go to the big city?" she asked.

"Sure," I replied.

"Woo hoo!" she cheered. "Okay, Uncle Levi, you may take me home."

Levi turned to Ella who shrunk away from him millimeter by millimeter. "Go ahead! I'll meet up with you later," Ella said. I saw pain course through his eyes.

"Yeah, sure. I'll call you when I get back," he said. Taking one last glance at Kady who stood stoically, he turned toward the outer barriers to take Winnie home. As he got away from the group, I looked at Dylan who nodded in return. I sprinted after Levi catching up with him and Winnie.

"You okay, Dublin?" I asked.

He stopped and turned to me. "I'm okay, Grace. I don't know what I was thinking coming with Ella. She couldn't stand the sight of Winnie. How could someone look at this angel like that?" he said grinning at her.

"Hell, if I know," she blurted out.

I covered my mouth with my hand to hide my laugh. As I regained my composure to scold her, Levi beat me to the punch. He sat her down, bending down before her. "Winnie, pretty little girls don't say hell. Okay?"

"I know, but I heard my momma say it a lot," she said.

"Yes, well, some adults say it. Even Aunt Grace," he said. I kicked him in the shin. "But you are supposed to be good until Christmas so Santa will come. Right?"

"I suppose," she said hanging her head.

"It's okay, sweetheart," he hugged her. "Just don't say it anymore, okay?"

"Yes, sir," she said.

He scooped her up again and turned to me. "Go tell him," he said.

"Levi!"

"Now, go!" he laughed as he carried Winnie to my truck.

Turning back to Dylan, he watched me return. He spoke to the preacher and his daughter, but kept his eyes on me.

Kady spoke to me first, "So, the curse is almost over, right?"

"Thankfully, yes. If I can make it to midnight," I said.

"I'm sorry for the way I've acted, Grace. I had no right," she said to me, but smiled at Dylan.

Part of me understood her hatred of me. If Dylan even hinted at liking another girl, I'd probably lose my sanity. "I understand, but I'm not the one that should get the apology."

She looked at her feet. She wore the cutest brown boots. "I'm not ready to swallow my pride on that one, yet," she said. "Maybe it's for the best."

Dr. Tabitha Mistborne walked up to us. "Hi, Grace, how are you feeling?"

"Official visit, Doc?" I asked.

"No, just checking on a friend," she replied.

Friend. I rarely had friends, much less female friends. "Thank you very much," I said looking at Dylan.

"Come this way. You need to try this fudge that Mrs. Frist made," she said pulling me away. Dylan continued to talk to the preacher and his daughter while the doctor led me toward the candy carts. Before we got to there, she said, "You aren't okay."

"Actually, I feel terrible. Every bit of power in me is draining," I said.

"You shouldn't be out here. Let Dylan take you home. Get out of the cold," she said.

I grimaced. I felt it was my duty to be there. If for no other reason than to prove that I'd beat this curse. "Dr. Mistborne, I need to stay," I said.

"Call me Tabitha, and I understand. Here take this," she said offering me a clear luminescent crystal. "It's storing some healing power. Perhaps it will come in handy to make it through the night."

I stared at the crystal as I took it from her. It brightened with my touch. "Wow!"

"It responds to your power. Just keep it in your pocket. It will know when you need it," she said.

"Thank you, Tabitha," I said.

"No problem. We should do lunch sometime," she said before walking away.

"Yes, we should," I said.

"Everything okay?" Dylan asked startling me from behind.

Spinning to meet his eyes, I realized how worried he was about me. "She gave me a crystal just in case."

"I'm taking you home," he said.

"Make me," I teased.

"I'm serious, Grace. I won't lose you now. You've already scared the crap out of me several times this week. Please, let me take you home," he begged.

Across the plaza, a man started screaming. "Oh, hell," I muttered.

Dylan's eyes turned to the scream like a hawk, then he bounded through the crowd toward the commotion. I followed, only slower. The heels on my boots prevented me from running. It occurred to me that we'd gone all day without a troll incident. We were due.

As the crowd cleared before me, BBQ Brad held a plump man down and screamed at him. The man's mouth was stuffed with sausages, and he couldn't speak.

"Brad, what happened?" Dylan asked.

"What's it look like Dylan? He's eating all my sausages," Brad whined.

I laughed, "Don't get your tinsel in a tangle, Brad. It's Christmas. Maybe he was starving."

He turned his mouth sideways looking down at the troll. "He ain't missed no meals."

"Hey!" the guy managed through a mouthful of sausage.

Troy Maynard sauntered up with Amanda and her son. "This must be Phillip."

"You know his name?" I asked.

"Yep. The brothers and I are getting to know each other," he smiled.

Two deputies grabbed Phillip up and dragged him to the nearest cruiser.

"Four more. Know anything about them? Or their mother?" I asked.

"Levi showed me the info he found online. The stories say their mother is a witch or an ogress," Troy said.

"Good grief," I grimaced. "Just what we need with the Cane Creek girls in town."

"I checked the Palmer place this morning. They've moved on," Troy said.

I shook my head. Knowing how far they travelled to get here, there was no way they'd cut and run.

"They are still here," Dylan said.

"How do you know that Mr. Lawman?" I asked playfully since I'd come to the same conclusion. Then I saw it, fear and anger furrowed his brow. I turned to look behind me. Four goth bitches walked toward us.

"Troy, clear the plaza," I said.

"Amanda, take Mark home," Troy instructed. With a loud voice, he turned to the crowd. "Everyone, please clear the plaza. We've had a credible threat, and I need everyone to move out quickly." In the world we lived in, the humans would turn on each other in acts of terrorism. The simple statement was enough to catch everyone's attention.

The people stood stunned for a moment, but quickly began to run in different directions. Watching the witches spread out before us, I pushed my sleeves up revealing my tattoo. I knew the curse was taking most of my power, but I would not let these woman hurt my town.

"I am Gloriana, Queen of the Exiles. I order you to leave this town at once. Everyone here is under my protection," I said loudly. Looking around, I noticed that a few of the townsfolk remained including my grandfather.

Lisette stopped her approach and smiled at me. "Misfit Queen in a town full of misfits. You are all a joke. Look at you, the curse eats at your soul. The more you fight it the more you lose yourself. Soon you will be dead."

"Last chance, swamp butt," I said. Dylan's warmth passed over me as he moved closer.

"I had to alter the curse once I saw you last night. My dolly had the wrong color hair." She pulled a misshapen handmade poppet from her pocket. Its hair had been ripped out, and she had glued a tuft of platinum hair to its head.

"Grace," Dylan began to panic.

"Real priestesses don't use dolls. It's a myth," I said.

"I'll show you a myth," Lisette laughed, "Now where's my boyfriend? I want him to see you die." What was it with Levi and his girls? They all hated me.

"You stay away from him," I growled as I unleashed the power in my tattoo. The spiraling filigree spread across my skin, as the jewel flashed a rich blue.

She cackled as the minions began to chant. Wrapping her forefinger and thumb around the doll's neck, she squeezed. My airway started to close. I gasped sucking in air.

Troy shifted to wolf form and bounded toward the doll. As his teeth nipped at the deformed charm, a wave of force hit him slamming him into Brad's BBQ cart.

I sank to my knees gasping for breath. Dylan hit his knees in front of me. His eyes filled with pain. He reached out to me, but I pulled away. "No, don't touch. Just let me go. Keep Levi safe."

"I can't let you go," he said. Spinning to his feet, his body erupted into flame. He rushed toward Lisette.

"No, Dylan, she is protected," I croaked.

With a few inches to spare, another wave of force hit Dylan extinguishing his flames and throwing him across the square. He slammed into a parked car. His limp form laid in the street.

"No," I gasped trying to stand. I pushed more power through the tattoo causing the grass and street to freeze. The full moon was covered by clouds as snow began to fall. Managing to make it to my feet, I threw my hand toward the witch to her right. As I suspected, they used their power to protect her leaving none for themselves. The caramel skinned woman froze into a solid block of ice.

Lisette laughed, tightening her grip. I stumbled, but threw power to the witch on her left who cubed nicely.

"I will kill them all, Lisette. Release me," I growled.

"No, filthy fairy whore, you only have moments left," she laughed.

She was right. The power I stored was depleted. I reached into my pocket, gripping the crystal that Tabitha gave me. It pulsed in my hand feeding power into me. A sudden surge of strength quickly waned, and the crystal winked out. It was only stubbornness that kept me alive now.

The light thrum of string music wafted through the air. I felt it approach me, surrounding my body like a blanket. The tune soothed me. Out of the darkness of the alley across the street, Levi approached. His eyes fixed on me. The music swelled spinning around me. The grip on my throat released as the hex was dispelled.

"Well, if it isn't the cutest Texan this side of the Mississippi," Lisette cooed. "Levi, honey, I know you've missed me."

"Shut-up, Lisette," he growled continuing to play. Despite being able to breathe, I had no magic left. Sitting on my knees, I saw Levi's eyes waiver from me to the witch. She twirled her hand in the air calling his attention.

"Your little song was so nice, but you aren't the only one who can enthrall," she said twirling her hand at the wrist.

"Levi, don't look at her hand," I sputtered.

He fixed his eyes on me, but his knees shook. Sinking to one knee, he continued to play, but the song faltered, and my air closed off again. My vision became blurry when a booming voice filled the air.

"You will not harm them," the male voice echoed off the surrounding buildings.

Krampus stood over Dylan's limp form.

"I am only claiming what is rightfully mine. Granted by your divine power, my Lord," Lisette said bowing to Deacon Giles in his towering Krampus form.

"You deceived me. Do you know what happens to people that deceive me?" he bleated.

"As your humble servant, I acknowledge your great power. I advise you to not cower to this weak excuse for royalty," she said pointing to me.

"Child. Arrogant child. Cease your machinations against my Queen," he ordered. "Or pay the price for defiance. I will cut off your power, your coven's power. Then I will snuff your insignificant life out," he said raising a hoof and slamming into down on one of the ice block witches. Bloody bits of ice exploded across the grass. The two unfrozen witches screamed breaking up their chant. They ran from the square leaving Lisette behind.

I gagged turning away from the bloody ice chunks. I'd done the same thing to some red caps, but they were fairies. This was a human woman. Her blood was on my hands. It made me a murderer. If Troy survived this, he would come after me.

Levi's song changed to a warm melody. The swirling around me ceased as I grasped at the last moments of my life. The ice surrounding the last witch began to melt. Levi didn't want to see another life end here. Bless him.

Focusing one last time on Dylan's limp form, tears streamed down my face. Regret clamped down on my heart. So many words left unsaid because of fear. He deserved so much better than me. I burned his heart over and over, but he just kept coming back. My heart was his, but I didn't tell him. I had to live to tell him.

"Release her now!" Deacon bellowed.

I heard a quiet gasp, and my lungs filled with air. Pushing myself off the ground, I looked to see Deacon holding Lisette by the neck, her feet dangling below her. The grotesque poppet laid on the ground. The frozen witch, now thawed, laid below on the ground, her chest slowly rising and falling. The other two huddled together behind the gazebo cowering from the goat demon.

Levi stopped playing, dropping his guitar to the ground and ran to me. "Are you okay?" he asked steadying me as I stood.

"Check Dylan," I muttered. He looked toward where Dylan had been thrown, and a pile of ash lay in the street.

"No," I sobbed.

"He will come back," Levi murmured. When Dylan died once before, I didn't know he was a Phoenix. Now, I wasn't sure what we needed to do. Would he just rise up?

"My Queen, would you like me to kill her?" Deacon asked.

The curse still wove its way through my veins, and I stumbled as I stepped toward Dylan's ashes. Levi took my hand and placed it firmly on his shoulder. Leaning into his chest, I swapped gravy with him once again. The euphoria wasn't the same. My eyes rolled back into my head as my body drank in the power. No erotic feelings pulsed over me. Just an eagerness to end this before any other lives were lost. Pulling my hand away, he muttered, "Geez, I felt it that time."

"Deacon, please put her down," he lowered her allowing her feet to touch the ground, but didn't release her neck.

The clock tower on city hall rang out. Twelve loud clangs from the bell inside the tower resounded in the plaza.

10

DECEMBER 21ST

THE CURSE FADED, AND MY STRENGTH RETURNED.

"Lisette Delphin, return to your swamp. I will employ my servants to track your every move. If you so much as step foot inside the state of Alabama again, I will ring your neck myself," I growled. "Do you understand?"

"Yes," she strained.

"Yes, what?" I prompted. Levi snickered behind me.

"Yes, my Queen," she said as a temporary smile crossed my face.

"Swear it by your power and your life," I pressed. The last thing I wanted to do was kill her. Even after all the crap she'd put Levi through. If she would swear this oath, then she would be bound by it. If she broke it, her magic would die.

"By the power of the generations of Cane Creek priestesses who proceeded me and by my own life's blood, I swear never to return to this state," she said.

"And?" I prompted again.

"And I promise to never curse you and yours ever again," she said.

I paced toward her, staring into her eyes. "Every exiled fairy on this planet is mine, do you understand?" I barked.

"Yes," she replied cowering.

"If he doesn't get up," I said pointing towards Dylan's ashes, "I will gladly break my oath forfeiting my life to end yours."

She nodded. I wrapped my cold hand around her wrist jerking her to the nearest tree. I requested that she be deposited somewhere in Louisiana, preferably in a swamp. The tree obliged, and she disappeared from sight.

"Deacon, go home. We will discuss the dead witch soon," I said.

"Yes, my Queen," he mumbled now back in his lowly farmer shape.

"Thank you, Deacon," I added. His eyes brightened, nodding before walking away.

I slowly approached the ashes when Nestor grabbed my arm. "No, leave it. It only takes a minute," he said.

His jacket and clothes laid in the pile. We stared in anticipation. Levi walked over to the naked form of Troy Maynard.

"He's alive," he said. I knew Troy would heal quickly with his lycanthropic abilities. Dr. Mistborne approached him with Amanda and Mark not far behind.

"I'll take care of him," Tabitha said as she patted her hand.

Levi stood with us as we waited. Another dark form exited the alley where he emerged from earlier. He made eye contact and waved Kady over to us.

"She came and got me as soon as she saw Lisette," he said, hugging her when she reached him.

"Thank you, Kady," I said.

She nodded. Mable approached and locked arms with Nestor. He leaned over and kissed the top of her head.

"So, Mable, to what extent do you spy for my father?" I dared to ask.

"Not the time, Grace," Nestor said.

"Fine," I growled.

A light wind swept past us stirring the ashes. They swirled above Dylan's clothes as streaks of fire joined the dust. The cyclone built in power until the ashes were nothing but flames. The warmth touched our faces as it emanated from the wind. It felt like him. It smelled like him.

I stepped toward it, but Nestor held me back. The spinning force was mesmerizing and beautiful. My hands covered my gaping mouth as the fire took the form of a large fire bird floating ten feet above the plaza. The wind stopped whirling, but pulsed toward us as the magnificent bird flapped its wings. Waves of heat melted the remaining snow from my earlier spell.

As the bird's claws touched the ground, they shifted to feet and legs. In an instant, Dylan's fiery form stood before us with outstretched wings. A smile crossed his face, and I melted.

The brunette trailer park queen snapped into place as I rushed toward him. He'd barely tucked the fiery wings and turned to flesh when my body collided with his.

"Damn, Grace. Let me at least put my pants on," he said.

I gave only as much space as it was necessary to shrug into his jeans before wrapping myself around him again.

"Stop dying," I said into his ear as his strong arms pulled me tighter to him.

"You are one to talk," he whispered in my ear sending chills down my spine. My arms erupted into goosebumps.

He pressed his forehead to mine. Touching his cheeks, I swallowed all the fear and apprehension that I had spent months fighting. I didn't want to fight it anymore. I gave into my heart. His eyes searched mine. "What's wrong?"

"Nothing," I said quietly.

"Do I need to ask for time to kiss you?"

"Yes," I said allowing the humor to dance through my eyes.

"I told you last time that I wanted forever," he said.

Brushing his cheek with my lips I said, "Granted."

He groaned pressing my body to his. Our lips tangled in the desperation and hunger that had built over the last few days. I nearly forgot we had an audience. Nearly.

I heard Levi chuckle, and Kady shushing him. I leaned back from Dylan's lips as he smiled. "Do you mean it?" he asked.

"Yes, because I love you," I admitted. A rush of withheld and denied emotions flowed out of me with relief as I looked into his stunned face. "You don't believe me."

"Say it again, just so I'm sure," he said.

"I'd rather just pinch you to prove that you aren't dreaming," I said.

He laughed, "You can do that, too."

"I love you, Dylan Riggs," I said clearly.

His lips met mine again. Quickly he pulled away, sucking on my bottom lip. The fairy whore inside of me exploded in delight. "I love you too, Grace."

He kissed me again, but only for a second, before picking up his jacket and other clothes. Then he locked his hand in mine tugging me across the plaza. His long strides pulled faster than my high heeled boots could handle.

"Hey, y'all," he said sweeping past our audience.

They all muttered a greeting amidst laughter. "Dylan, I'm going to fall in these boots!" I exclaimed. He turned to me with passion and mischief in his eyes. Scooping me up, he threw me over his shoulder. "Oh my god! Dylan put me down!" I pounded his back with my flimsy fists. I heard the rumble of laughter in his chest.

"Don't keep her out too late! Use protection," Levi called after us. I blushed. What a goof.

"Don't wait up, Levi," Dylan hollered, as I flipped Levi the bird. They all laughed.

My blush deepened. "Where are we going, Dylan?"

"Home," he smiled as he opened the door to the Camaro. I slid in not understanding his meaning. Surely, he didn't mean his house. I'd never been to his property.

Nestor once told me that Dylan owned a lot of land and a significant house that he once shared with Stephanie. He'd never taken me there, but I didn't question it. I just assumed he didn't want me there because of his past with her. Hell, I didn't care where he took me as long as there was nudity and lovemaking.

❄

Turning down a road I'd never been on, the forest grew thick on both sides of the unpainted road. We approached an iron gate with no frills or markings. It slowly opened as we approached.

"Did you press a button to make it open?" I asked.

Without looking at me he smiled and said, "No, it's Bluetooth controlled to my phone. It knows it's me."

"Well damn, look at you all tech savvy," I teased. He slid his hand into mine and squeezed.

The road narrowed to one lane. The forest thinned to rolling pasture. I could only see the foundation of the house and the base of white columns because the road was lined with ancient oak trees. Something inside of me stirred, wanting to touch all of them.

The view cleared the closer we got to the house. A two-story antebellum house rose from a stone foundation. The stark white columns illuminated the front of the house as the moon reflected off of them. Dylan cut his eyes to me watching my expression.

Frankly, I was blown away. Dylan Riggs lived in a mansion. The enormous house made me feel small. Shifting in my seat, I looked away from the house. The field spread wide with a dirt drive leading to a large barn.

"You don't like it," he mumbled.

"It's amazing, but…" I paused trying to use my words carefully. Something I generally didn't do, however the last thing I wanted to do was fight with him.

"But what?" he prompted as the door of the garage behind the house slowly lifted. He pulled the Camaro into its spot beside a large F150 almost identical to mine. It was royal blue.

"You have a truck?" I asked distracted by the gleaming blue beast.

He chuckled, "Yes, I use it here on the property."

"It looks just like mine," I said.

"Remember the day that you met me out at the Drish farm?" he asked.

The memory washed over me of several of the guys in the department, Dylan and myself chasing loose livestock. "The hobgoblin," I recalled that the little shit kept letting the animals back out the moment we got them rounded up. Mrs. Drish's husband had died earlier that year, and she relied on paid help to manage the farm. However, when the animals kept getting out, the help called for help.

"You scared the crap out of him, and he agreed to move on instead of you unleashing your wrath. You were downright scary. I was impressed," he laughed as he turned off the car.

"I wouldn't have killed him or anything," the last word escaped my lips, and the death of the witch in the plaza hit me. I bolted out of the car. My chest heaved as my hands shook. I'd taken out plenty of evil fairies, but never a human.

Dylan circled the car in a panic. "What's wrong? Grace, talk to me," he begged as he placed his warm palms on my cheeks.

"I didn't mean for her to die," I said clasping his wrists.

"Who?"

"The witch in the plaza," I muttered as the vision of bloody ice bits flashed through my brain.

He stared at me confused. He was already down when Deacon smashed her. I waited for condemnation, but all I saw in his eyes was worry.

"One of the ones that killed me?" he asked making a point of their own treachery.

I nodded. "I froze two of them, because they were supplying power to Lisette. Deacon became Krampus and smashed her."

"Deacon killed her," he said.

"But I froze her," I said.

"Grace, you never meant for her to die. Did you?"

I shook my head. "But I need to be more aware that my actions have consequences. I can't lose myself."

"Despite all your protests to the contrary, I know you have a big heart. You've taken this queen responsibility far more seriously than I gave you credit for. However, you need to remember that protecting us may mean that you have to take down some very powerful humans. Those women wanted us all dead. You managed to subdue them with only one life lost," he said.

"Two," I muttered. He ran his finger down my edge of my jaw.

"Two," he confirmed pulling me into his arms. His lips traced the same pattern along my jaw. I moaned at the warmth of his body and the softness of his lips. The faith he had in me blew me away. I was not sure I'd ever understand it. He pulled away taking my hand. He led me into the kitchen of the home, which was modernized contrary to its outward appearance. Deep cherry cabinets and black marble countertops. All of it impeccably clean.

"You fell asleep in your truck," he said out of the blue. He pulled two cans of soda out of the stainless-steel refrigerator handing me one.

"Oh, at the Drish place," I replied picking up with the previous conversation.

"Yes, after you talked to the hobgoblin, I told you to sit in the truck while we double checked all the gates, and I'd follow you home. It was very late. We were all exhausted. When I finished talking to Mrs. Drish, I found you asleep. I had one of the guys drive my cruiser back, and I took you home."

"I woke up in my bed trying to figure out how I got home," I said talking a sip of the cool drink. "I called you, and you played dumb."

He laughed. "You were so confused. I never went back and explained it to you. I just assumed you realized that I took you home. But, anyway, I liked your truck so much that I bought one."

"You bought a truck just like mine? That's creepy, Dylan," I said.

"Mine's newer and nicer than yours," he smirked.

"Well, excuse me," I returned.

He offered his hand. I took it as he guided me into a large den with soft leather couches and a beautiful stone fireplace. The house definitely had his masculine touch.

In a display of power, which I'd never seen from him besides rising from the dead, he pointed to the fireplace, and it erupted in flame. "Shit," I mumbled.

The flames illuminated with soft amber light, warming the cool space almost immediately. He sat on the couch, pulling me to him. I straddled his lap kissing his bare neck. He slipped his warm hands under my sweater pulling it off over my head.

"I've wanted you so badly since that first time," he whispered as he nibbled on my ear.

"I wanted it too, but it was against my rules," I replied back as he unhooked my bra.

"Stupid rules," he murmured.

"Yes," I agreed. He pushed me up off of him to his side. My back hit the couch as he lunged over me. I squealed, because he caught me off guard. Reaching to unbutton his pants, he stopped me. He proceeded to find numerous places on my body to kiss, setting me on fire and building the tension. It was like playing pool all over again, just a different game. Dylan was damn good at games.

He brushed my cheeks with the stubble on his face. I giggled and jerked from him. He grinned as we wrestled until he pinned me with a deep, soft kiss. I moaned, "Please stop torturing me."

"Revenge, my love," he laughed, as he held me in place.

"I suppose I deserve it," I admitted.

"Mmm, yes, you do," he said. Releasing me he stood, his fingers beckoned me to follow him. So, I did through the moonlit house, up a twisting stairwell and down a long hallway. He opened the double doors to a darkened room. Pushing me in to the darkness, he pressed up behind me. The doors clicked shut. I felt his warm breath on my neck as he wrapped an arm around my waist.

"I've waited so long, Grace, to bring you to my home, to my bed. I hope you like it," he breathed. I felt his heart pounding in his chest with a slight tremor in his body. He was nervous. It wasn't like this was our first roll in the hay. I shifted uneasily in the darkness. I trusted him, but the anticipation of something happening flowed through me like lava. Or maybe that was just Dylan.

I felt him move the arm that wasn't circling my waist. One by one candles placed all around the room flickered to life. Every surface in the room was covered in pillar candles. All different sizes lined up on the dresser, end tables, window sills, and in clusters on the floor.

"Oh my," I gasped. Every sexual experience in my life up to this had been a "wham, bam, thank you, ma'am." Which I was fine with because it allowed me to guard my emotions, keeping every partner away from my heart. This was different, almost as if it were the first time.

The room wasn't as masculine as the lower level of the house. Muted tones gave it a soft and welcoming feel. The large wooden bed, covered in pillows and a fluffy comforter, was inviting.

His kissed my shoulder as I looked in awe. "Forgive me for not inviting you here before, but I remodeled the whole house after she left. I purged all of it in hopes that one day you would finally give in to me."

I turned to face him. Heaven forbid I let something go. "The night we took the first brother to the jail. You had the chance then to have me, but you didn't," I said, kissing his chest.

A small laugh escaped his lips. "The remodel wasn't done until two days ago. I wanted to bring you here."

"Romantic fool," I said poking him in the stomach. I winced in pain because his stomach was ripped. There were so many days I watched him pace my lawn with his shirt off, cutting my grass.

"See, you hurt yourself," he teased, bringing my finger to his mouth and sucking on it. I darted across the room, and he chased me to the bed. The wrestling match ended with me on top holding him down. Right where he wanted me because he grinned.

"You devil," I said reminding us both if that first night. The words had barely left my mouth when the game ended, and we got lost in each other until morning.

The sun streamed through gauzy curtains as I awoke tangled up with Dylan. He still slept. Honestly, I thought that perhaps the morning after would be like the last one. Appreciative of the experience, but instant regret. However, that ominous feeling never crossed my mind or my heart. Everything felt right about being in his arms.

I was intimidated by his big house and apparent wealth. He'd never hinted at such a thing before. He remodeled the entire house just to wipe away all the memories of his time with Stephanie. In a way, I understood the sentiment. I also knew that he felt like he needed to impress me. But, hell, a cottage or cabin would impress a girl who lived in a double wide.

Dylan looked at me differently. Despite him calling me trailer trash, he looked at me like a queen. I only saw myself as a misfit until recently. Even with all the havoc caused by the trolls plus the witches, I finally found a place where I fit. Currently, that place was in his arms.

The candles had all died out, but the smell of melted vanilla wax hung in the room. For a few moments, I allowed myself to imagine living in this big house. I didn't know what his plans were for us, but I decided I'd let him guide the way. Being in a relationship would be a whole new experience for me. I had no idea where to start, but I certainly didn't want to start by assuming that this house would ever be home.

"Good morning, Grace," he mumbled, pulling me tighter to him.

"Mornin' Darlin'," I replied.

He grunted, "Oh god, I love hearing you say it."

"Seems like a bland choice to me," I teased. "Pookie was so much better."

"I never want to hear that name again," he laughed. "Besides it's not bland. I've heard your real accent, my dear, and intriguing as it is, when you turn up the southern, I start losing space in my pants."

Laughing at him, I said, "Here I thought it was my charm and good looks."

"Those aren't bad, either," he said. "I'm gonna make coffee. There is a bathroom right over there if you want to shower. And that closet has clothes in it for you."

"You bought clothes? For me?" I asked.

"I don't think you realize how long I've been planning to trap you here," he said as he rose out of the bed. I stared at every magnificent inch of him.

"I'm going to ignore that creepy comment and beg you to come back to bed," I said.

"What about coffee?" he pointed over his shoulder.

"If you'd rather have coffee than morning sex, then go ahead, Dylan," I said, pulling the comforter off of me to show him what he was turning down.

"Fuck," he groaned.

"No, fuck me," I purred.

"Yes, ma'am," he obeyed crawling back into the bed, and pulling the comforter over our heads. His damn smile. His warm hands. His body pressed to mine. Lord, have mercy.

I showered in the biggest bathroom I'd ever seen. The shower and the bathtub were separate. The shower had frosted glass walls and slick tan tiles. The tub, which I hoped to use some day, was a large iron claw foot. An antique piece in a modernized antique house.

Stalker Dylan had all the products I liked in the bathroom. I shook my head. At least, he was paying attention.

In the closet, I found a selection of clothes much like the ones I already owned except less two-bit whore. I pulled on a very expensive pair of soft jeans, and a loose tan sweater.

As I passed through the house, I peeked into the rooms, but not entering them or wandering off the direct path to the kitchen. Upstairs were mostly bedrooms, except for a very manly study. The downstairs were covered in dark wood floors and soft rugs.

Standing at the kitchen sink, he wore a white t-shirt that hugged his muscles and a pair of long hung cotton pants. He handed me a cup of coffee. As his hand brushed mine, I shivered.

"You cold?"

"No," I muttered sipping my coffee.

He sat his on the counter and leaned over smelling my freshly washed hair. "So, just my touch makes you tremble," he teased.

"Dream on, Dylan Riggs," I denied. Deny. Deny. Deny.

"I bet that's not all it does," he grinned.

"Whatever," I replied.

"What do you think of the house?" he asked.

"It's wonderful. Thank you for sharing it with me," I said.

"Who are you? And what have you done with my Grace?" he said.

"I can be nice, occasionally," I rebutted him. "Don't get used to it."

I heard my phone ringing over on the couch. It must have fallen out of my pocket while we wrestled last night.

"It's Levi," Dylan said as I went to answer it.

"How do you know?"

"It rang twice while you were in the shower," he said. "I didn't answer it."

"You could have answered it. I don't care," I said as I answered it. "Hello."

"Really? You make fun of me for a few hours, but you've been gone all night," Levi teased.

"Shut your mouth, Levi Rearden. What do you want?"

"Winnie wants to know if you are still taking her shopping?" he said. I could hear cartoons in the background.

"Crap. I almost forgot. Tell her I'll be back in a few minutes," I said.

"Alright. At least take a shower, and wash the Dylan off you," he suggested.

I hung up on him. Looking at Dylan, he had turned to the sink and was washing out his cup. "Winnie?" he asked.

"Yes, I promised to take her shopping," I said as I leaned on the counter next to him. "Will you take me home?"

"Sure. If you will give me a few minutes, I'll take a quick shower and go shopping too. I need to make a few Christmas purchases," he said pressing his body on mine. He kissed me with sugary coffee lips. He tasted amazing. I needed to start putting sugar in my coffee.

"If you keep doing that we will never make it back to get Winnie," I said.

"Come here. I want show you something before we go." He dragged me back upstairs and instead of turning to the left toward the master bedroom. He turned right, opening the first door.

Inside was a child's wonderland room. Painted girly colors with rainbows and unicorns. A large white iron bed with gauzy drapes around it. Fit for a princess. A bookshelf lined with story books. A toy box open and ready to be filled. "Dylan, what is this?"

"I know how much she means to you, and maybe we can bring her out here. She would love the animals. I'll have a new foal soon, and I thought she would need a room to play in or take a nap. I've seen her room in that trailer. It's awful," he muttered.

Tears rolled down my cheeks. It was beautiful. The kind of room a real father would make for his child. "You have to be the most amazing man on earth," I said.

"I will remind you often that those words came out of your mouth, and you meant them," he teased. "Don't cry, baby."

He wiped the tears, as he kissed my cheek. "Thank you, Dylan."

"Good grief, I'm beginning to think that some angel possessed you last night with all these sweet words," he laughed as he headed toward the master bedroom.

"I'll get my head on straight soon," I said staring at his ass as he walked down the hallway. "Well, maybe not."

He laughed, because he heard me.

"Please tell me you told him," Levi said quietly as he stood next to me in the mall. We watched Winnie sitting on Santa's lap telling him what she wanted for Christmas. Dylan paid for the picture, so I could hang it on my fridge.

"None of your business, Dublin," I said.

"Good, it's about time," he smirked. I smacked him in the shoulder, but it didn't faze him. He just laughed at me. Dylan caught the exchange and grinned at us.

"You like the house?" he asked.

I turned to him and put my hands on my hips. "Levi, what do you know about that house?"

"I helped him with some of it. He paid me," he said.

"When was this?" I asked. "Because the last time I checked all you do is sleep with Kady."

"That's not true. I eat too," he laughed. "No, he asked me to come help, and on the days you would disappear. I'd go help him. Where were you by the way?"

"Spending time with my grandfather," I replied. Nestor and I had spent a lot of time together in the small apartment above the bar. I was trying to learn from his kind and open ways. He had a vast knowledge of fairies. He shared it all with me.

Winnie ran off the platform from Santa, jumping into Levi's

arms, "Uncle Levi! He said I'd been good, and he would bring me lots of Christmas presents!"

"You have been good. I'm sure you will get whatever you want," he said.

"You want a candy cane? He gave me two!" she said.

"Sure, let's go to the toy store, and you can show me what you want," he said.

"You have money?" I asked.

"Yes, Grace," he grumbled. Winnie laughed at him. Dylan traced his finger from my elbow to my hand. He planted a soft kiss on my cheek.

"She's so excited," he laughed.

"She's making me excited. I wonder if we could convince Bethany to let her spend the night at the trailer and open presents with us?"

He grimaced, but said, "Perhaps."

"What's wrong?" I asked.

"As long as we are together on Christmas, I'm not sure I care who else is there. If Winnie is there that's great. Levi can take a hike. What was he bothering you about?"

"What do you think?"

"Us?" he asked.

"No, not necessarily. He's been adamantly pushing me to tell you how I've felt. Besides, he told me your dirty little secret."

"What secret?"

"That you were paying him to help you on the house," I said.

His laughter filled the air around us. "Oh, *that* secret. I thought he'd told you about my secret dungeon full of fairy misfits."

"Or the secret relationship the two of you have been hiding from me," I teased.

"You will just have to share me with Levi and the dungeon," he teased back.

"As the queen, I would have to punish you for harming my subjects," I reminded him as we walked through the mall. Shoppers passed all round us, carrying red and green bags. The smell of roasted peanuts and cotton candy filled the air. Demonstrators stood at the center kiosks beckoning shoppers to sample or test their wares. I leaned into Dylan's warm frame, and he hummed with pleasure.

I spied the toy store up ahead, but Dylan pulled me to an empty bench. I sat next to him. "What would you like for Christmas, Grace?"

"I've been naughty," I said.

"This is true. I've seen it with my own eyes," he said as those eyes twinkled.

Clearing my throat, I said, "I thought I'd save Santa the trip."

The humor in his eyes faded, turning dark. He gripped my hand staring behind me. "No, don't look," he said barely breathing.

"Dylan, what is it?"

"Her," he said. Shaking his head, his body tensed. I knew she was coming toward us.

"Good afternoon, Dylan. It's Grace, right?" she smirked. "Glad you aren't dead, Dylan."

Her midnight hair glistened under the twinkling lights. The only thing with more twinkle was the giant diamond on her finger. Looking at her through my sight, her features enhanced with large eyes and pointed ears. Stephanie was royal born elf. Seelie fairy. Sworn enemies of my father's wild fairies. I hated her on principle.

"I wasn't dead. It was an operation to discover the individuals responsible for killing those children," he explained. I'd never thought what the explanation was for the external world. Those of us who knew the truth about Shady Grove and its inhabitants never questioned Dylan's reappearance. The rest of the world saw the panicked videos from the courthouse with a dead man on a sidewalk. I knew that Stephanie was a high-born elf, but perhaps the reappearance of Mr. Riggs hadn't reached outside of our town.

The reason we couldn't get any info about his death early on was that at the scene the body had disappeared. The Sanhedrin had something to do with a distraction that allowed Dylan to rise without the watchful eyes of normal humans.

"I've got to find Sergio. He wandered off while I was shopping. Have you seen him?" she asked Dylan. Sergio Krykos, her boyfriend, was the head partner of a large law firm in Tuscaloosa. His Greek heritage was very apparent the day I first saw him at Dylan's memorial service. She'd consistently cheated on Dylan with her boss, and now apparently, she was engaged to him.

"No, I haven't seen him," he said squeezing my hand. His eyes rested on the diamond.

"Oh, we haven't officially announced it, but isn't the ring gorgeous?!" she said pushing the diamond toward my face.

"It's lovely," I responded.

"So, you are fucking Dylan now? Or were you always fucking him? Does your daddy know?" she said pointedly.

Dylan stood up pulling me with him. He paced away from her as she laughed. He continued to walk to the far end of the mall. I jerked his hand to grab his attention. "Dylan, stop. Darlin' we've run far enough."

He turned quickly wrapping me in his arms. I knew Dylan loved me, but she had a way of hurting him that I didn't expect. His breathing slowed. "She stuck that in your face, and I wanted to strangle her. You were too kind, Grace," he said.

"You were worried about me?" I asked.

He sighed, "Yes, we just…"

I pulled his chin up to look into his eyes, "We didn't just. We have been us for a long time, even when she lived in your house. It was us, right?"

"It felt like it was only me," he said.

Looking back over the past five years from the moment I met Dylan, so many people told me what we were, and I ignored it. Chris Purcell told me. Nestor, my grandfather, told me. Jeremiah told me. Hell, it only took Levi seeing us once to tell me. I'd wanted Dylan for much longer than I cared to admit.

"It wasn't," I said. His mouth covered mine with a sweet, gentle kiss. Public displays of affection were a huge no-no in my old rule book. I burned that book.

"Ew, get a room," Levi said.

"Ew, get a room," Winnie echoed.

I started laughing. Dylan joined me. "You finished shopping, Winnie?" Levi carried multiple bags. Mostly new clothes and a nice new coat for Winnie.

"I suppose if I decide I need anything else, Uncle Levi will bring me back," she said.

"Lordy, child," I said taking her hand. She grinned as we walked out of the mall to my black truck.

Nightfall came quickly, and Winnie decided to spend the night. Levi went over to talk to Bethany about it. When he returned, his face was dark.

"What's wrong?" I asked.

"Not now," he said looking at Winnie who was finishing up a Christmas scene to hang on my fridge.

She held up for me to see. "Oh, Winnie, it's beautiful!" Her tiny fingers had drawn a Christmas tree with four figures. Dylan, Levi, Grace and Winnie. A furry dog sat next to her figure. An awkward family, but still a family.

"Where's Kady?" I asked Levi.

"Her family had a gathering tonight," Levi answered.

"You weren't invited?" I asked.

"Everything is fine with us. It was a private thing," he said assuring me that I didn't need to worry or kill Kady, whichever the circumstance demanded.

"Winnie! Bedtime!" I announced. She groaned but kissed

everyone good night. She gave extra hugs to Rufus who wagged his tail around our feet. Levi took her to the front room to read a bedtime story. Dylan helped me clear the crayons from the table.

"You said earlier that you wanted to get a shower. Go ahead. I'll clean up," he offered kissing me on the cheek.

"You staying tonight?" I asked not wanting to assume.

"Grace, I never want to spend another night without you," he said.

"Stop being so damn romantic. Makes me feel completely inadequate," I protested.

He smiled, "You make up for it in other ways."

I opened my mouth to say something else smart, but clamped it shut as he laughed at me. Shutting the bedroom door, I wasn't trying to keep Dylan out. I just didn't want Levi seeing me naked. So many of my sentiments had changed. Levi had *accidentally* seen me several times in my underwear. It didn't bother me then. Now it did.

Despite fairies basically being whores, once they made a commitment to another fairy they remained faithful. Beings like Levi's father took that loyalty to an extreme, even past death. I knew the feeling. Dylan was all I wanted.

Stripping out of my clothes, goosebumps spread across my arms with an uneasy feeling. A nagging thought tugged at my brain. No troll. The day was almost over and the next one hadn't appeared. I wrapped a towel around me, peeking out the door.

Dylan stood at the counter drinking coffee. His eyes met mine. "What's wrong?"

"Call Troy. We are missing a troll," I said.

"Ugh! You're right. I'll take care of it. Go shower," he urged.

My desire for a long relaxing shower faded. Instead, I jumped in to quickly wash my hair. As I stepped out of the shower, my goosebumps and uneasy feeling returned. After drying off my body, I turned to the mirror wiping the fog off with my towel.

Putting the towel over my head, I massaged it through my hair drying small bits at a time. Finally, I looked up to assess my appearance in the mirror. My eyes met two black beady eyes staring back at me from the window behind me.

I screamed frantically wrapping the towel around my nude body. He stood in the window sniggering, not attempting to hide his presence. Dylan bounded into the bedroom as I rushed out of the bathroom and we collided. Both of us hit the floor in a heap of tangled limbs.

"He's outside looking in the window," I managed to choke out as Levi ran into the room.

"At least shut the door, damn y'all," Levi smirked.

"Troll! Outside!" Dylan growled at him. "Catch him, Levi."

It took a moment for him to register the command, but turned in his heels rushing to the front door.

Dylan touched my face. "Put on clothes, and please stay inside," he growled pushing himself up off the floor. As he exited the room, I grabbed the closest articles of clothing to me. Which were the clothes I took off before the shower. Wrestling them on my partially wet body, I heard Dylan yelling outside.

Once I was dressed, I heard the crunch of a fist on flesh. I took off to the front yard where Levi had the troll wrapped up as Dylan punched him repeatedly.

"Mercy! Mercy!" he begged. His eyes centered on me where I stood on the porch.

I descended the stairs quickly, but approached the enraged Dylan cautiously. "Darlin' you've pounded his face enough," I said.

"Not nearly," he growled, as he landed one last punch in his gut. The troll doubled over, and Levi let him hit the ground. "Stay down, you pervert."

"Dylan, calm down. It's not the first time someone's seen me naked," I said. Poor choice of words.

He swiveled to face me. "It's what he said," he explained as his blue eyes burned with anger. I placed my hand over his split knuckles pushing power through them to heal. His anger eased.

"It was pretty bad, Grace," Levi said.

"All I said was," the troll started, but Dylan spun back to him. He never finished the sentence, but stared at me. Actually, it was more of a leer. Like he was undressing me in his mind. He cowered below Dylan.

"Call Troy and get him out of here. I'm not even amused anymore," I said. Dylan fished out his phone. When Troy answered, Dylan stepped away a few feet to explain the situation.

"Your skin is so beautiful," the troll said.

"Hush up," I said to him.

"I'm in love with you," he continued.

"I told you to shut your mouth," I growled as Levi popped him on the head.

"I need a hug," he said as he lifted his arms begging for an embrace.

Levi shoved him face down into the cold grass. Dylan hung up the phone barreling toward the lewd menace.

I put my hands up. "It's not worth it, Dylan. Please."

"You would protect even him?" he shot at me.

"I'm protecting you," I said softly leaning into his chest. His tension eased, but only for a moment.

"He can't love you like I can," the troll said. Levi jerked him up, and Dylan shoved me out of his arms. With the crack of his fist on bone, the troll fell limp at their feet.

Dylan flexed his hand staring at the bloody split skin that I had just healed. Shaking my head, I turned to go back inside. "I told you to stay inside. You cannot just do as I asked. Not even once."

I ignored him. He wasn't mad at me. He was mad at himself for losing control. I'd been there and done that. Instead of hashing it out, I went inside to check on Winnie.

11

DECEMBER 22ND

SITTING IN THE DARKNESS ON THE END OF THE BED WHERE WINNIE slept, I envied her. She had slept through the whole debacle. Along the edges of the blinds, the blue lights of Troy's cruiser flickered. I heard muffled voices, then the lights faded as Troy hauled the brother to meet his kin.

"Two more," I sighed.

Hearing both of the men return, I eased off the bed and slipped out of the room. Dylan emerged from my bedroom confused, but then saw me and sighed.

Levi looked around the corner at me. "She okay?" he asked.

"Slept through all of it," I said.

I walked into the kitchen, grabbed a glass and filled it with tap water. After taking a sip, I asked Dylan, "What did Troy have to say about Peeping Tom?"

"Richard. Peeping Richard," Levi corrected with a smile hoping to ease the tension.

"He's a dick!" Dylan exclaimed.

I snorted, then laughed. Levi joined me, and finally the fire in Dylan's eyes died out. He put his hands in his front jean pockets. His head dropped, but bobbed with laughter. He reached a hand toward me, so I obliged him with mine. He pulled me to him and whispered, "Sorry."

"I'm not mad at you," I admitted. Most of my anger with Dylan since we first slept together was fake, anyway. I didn't want to spend precious time arguing with him. I guided him into the bedroom, clicking the door shut to give us privacy, as much as Levi who would spend the night on the couch.

He shook his head. "I'm convinced you are some fairy duplicate of my Grace. Your father body swapped you."

"I'm the me you always said I was. The fairy with a heart. And you can punch, fight and argue all you want, but it doesn't matter."

"Why?"

"Because in the end, I love you no matter what you do," I explained.

He groaned latching his mouth to mine. His lips worked slowly with mine. I could not get enough of him. Suppressing a moan, I pulled at his clothes. "Levi," he whispered.

"Oh, you are kissing me and thinking of him?" I teased.

"No, he will hear us," he laughed with his forehead pressed to mine.

"I've endured his romps with Kady for months. I dare him to say anything," I muttered.

That's all it took to convince him. He pulled his shirt off, then removed my sweater. I bit my lip as he breathed and nibbled my ear.

We spent several hours trying to provoke the other into making noise. Teasing and muffled love making, Dylan and I both cemented our names on the naughty list.

The sun hadn't been up long when Dylan woke me up. "Hey, I've got some errands to run today. Last minute stuff for the house. You want to go with me?"

"Actually, I've got a few things to do myself. I didn't buy gifts for Mable and Nestor, so I need to run back to town," I said.

"Are you taking Levi with you?" he asked.

"If he wants to go, I don't know what his plans are for today," I replied as he ran his finger across my eyebrows and down my cheeks. Despite his warm body heating the entire bed, a chill ran down my body. His touch drove me crazy, and he knew it. The bastard.

He got out of the bed parading around my room naked as a jaybird. I could get used to seeing naked Dylan every morning. Part of me didn't want to latch on to the idea that this was a permanent arrangement. He said forever, but I'm not so sure that was realistic. He was more romantic than me. He watched me admiring him, but he didn't acknowledge it or make a smart remark. Ducking into the bathroom, I saw that perfect ass right before the door shut.

I groaned.

"Torture, my love," he said.

"I hate you," I said.

"No, you don't," he said as the water in the shower turned on.

"Quite the opposite," I mumbled.

Grabbing a pair of shorts and a t-shirt, I found Levi still asleep on the couch which was unusual for him. Generally, he was always up before me. I thought it was because he worked on a farm back in Texas. He'd get up early in the morning to start chores before heading to school. He stirred when I came into the room.

"Hey sleepy head," I said starting the pot for coffee.

He groaned and pulled a blanket over his head. "I'm so tired," he said. "I need to take Winnie home."

"Yeah, please check on Bethany. I'm worried about her," I said.

Winnie must have heard us talking, and she came out of the bedroom wiping her eyes.

"Morning, Sweet Pea," I greeted her.

"Grits," she moaned.

"As you wish, Princess," I replied as I retrieved supplies to fill her belly before sending her home.

"Levi, get up," Winnie said pulling the blanket off his head. He howled in protest. She giggled until he reached to tickle her. Then she started shrieking. It was loud, but I let them have their fun. Dylan stepped out of the bedroom with a wet head. He laughed at them.

"Mr. Dylan, make Levi stop!" Winnie petitioned him.

"Levi, stop tickling her," Dylan scolded.

"No!" Levi defied him. Rufus got into it by barking at Levi. He loved Winnie, so naturally the pup was on her side.

"Stop! I'm gonna pee pee on you," Winnie cried.

Levi immediately stopped and put her down. She took several steps away from him. Put her hands on her hips as her chest heaved from the exertion. "Gotcha!" she laughed.

He lunged for her from his position on the couch. Missing her by inches, he plopped on the living room floor. We all had a good laugh at his expense. He stomped off to the bathroom grinning the whole way.

After breakfast, Levi took Winnie home. Dylan kissed me goodbye and went off to do his errands.

"Levi, how was Bethany?"

"She's on something bad. She was fine just now. Very talkative and alert. However, I've not seen her this thin," he said.

I didn't know what I could do to help the situation. Honestly, Winnie's well-being was my only concern. I picked up my phone and dialed my lawyer.

"Blake and Associates, how may I help you?" the receptionist answered.

"Hi, this is Grace Bryant. May speak to Mr. Remington Blake, please."

"One moment, Miss Bryant," she said as the phone clicked play garbled classical music.

"Grace?" Remy answered with his New Orleans accent.

"Good morning, Remy," I replied.

"Good? Actually the morning has been awful, but now I'm finer than a frog's hair split three ways hearing your sweet voice. How are you, honey?" he asked. Remy and I had a fling a few years back right before I moved to Shady Grove. He failed to tell me he was married, and once I found out, I moved from his side of town to here. We reconciled, however, he clearly wanted to revisit our former arrangements. I wasn't interested.

"Did you check on the paperwork for Wynonna Jones?" I asked ignoring his flirt.

"I did. Lysander completed everything perfectly. He didn't deceive you on that," he replied. After the confrontation with Lysander last year, I questioned every legal matter he attended to on my behalf. Remy volunteered to check everything for me. "In fact, all of it looked to be in order."

"Thank you, Remy," I said.

"Are you busy today? Let me take you to lunch," he offered.

"I've got some last-minute Christmas shopping to do, but Remy, you know I'm with Dylan," I said.

He sighed, "No, you are playing games with him."

"Actually, we've reconciled our differences, and we are together," I said driving the point home. Remy was gorgeous and a flirt, but he needed to know that my heart belonged to Dylan.

"I see," he said. "Congratulations, honey. When he disappoints you, I'll be here."

I started to reply, but the phone clicked off. He'd hung up. I hated to put it bluntly, but I needed him to know.

"He doesn't give up," Levi said.

"He means well," I said.

"Well, you have a fall back guy," Levi teased.

I groaned. He was right. I don't think that there would ever come a day that if I wanted Remington Blake that he would refuse me.

"Did you say you were going shopping again?" Levi asked.

"Yeah, I need to buy a few things. When you were working on Dylan's house, did he give you access to the security?" I asked.

"Um, why? Are you breaking into your boyfriend's house?" he asked. "Just ask him, he will let you in."

I sighed at the dense headed bard, "It's hard to surprise him if I ask ahead of time."

"Well, why didn't you say so? I took your truck over there one day, and he put a chip in it so the gate and garage doors would open for me. I have the code for the security system," he said.

I shook my head. Dylan never mentioned it, even after being at his house. I needed to think of some torture for this lack of disclosure. "I'm going to jerk a wart on him," I said.

"Warts are nasty, Grace!" Levi teased. "So, do I get to be in on the secret?"

"Yes, if you are ready to go, we can head out," I said.

"Where are you?" I texted Dylan after the day of shopping with Levi. He sat with me in the truck just down the road from the gate to Dylan's property.

I waited for thirty agonizing seconds when he answered, "I'm at the bar with Nestor. Come have some coffee."

"Levi and I are still out," I replied trying not to tell a direct lie. If I'd been in Ice Queen form, I probably would have spilled the beans right there.

"Okay. Call me when you get back in town," he said.

"I will. I love you," I texted back.

The phone rang. I laughed. So damn romantic. "Hello," I answered.

"I love you, too," he said and hung up.

"You guys are ten times worse than Kady and I ever were," Levi said. "And you are both ancient."

"Yeah, but this is the first time we've ever done this sort of thing," I defended our actions. I dialed the bar quickly.

"Hot Tin Roof," Nestor answered.

"Keep him there. Do not let him leave. If he does, you call me," I said.

"Um, okay," Nestor replied.

"Thanks. Don't call me by my name. I don't want him to know it's me," I said.

"I think you have the wrong number," Nestor said.

"Brilliant!" I said and hung up. "Let's do this."

Levi was excited about my plan, and I was glad to have him come along. Some things I bought were quite big which I needed strong man arms to lift. I backed up to the garage door as it lifted open. Levi jumped out to turn off the security system. I hoped he didn't have some fancy security system where his phone would notify him of motion or the alarm being turned off.

We spent over an hour turning Dylan's living room into the perfect setting for a Christmas postcard. The 10-foot tree stood in the corner just off the fireplace. It was adorned with red, gold and green ornaments glittering in the twinkling lights. I'd hung ever-green garland around the fireplace. Levi hung stockings for all of us, even Rufus.

Standing back and surveying the room, I asked Levi, "Well, is it too much?"

"He will love it," Levi said.

"I hope so," I sighed. "Let's get out of here before we get caught."

"Why don't you stay and surprise him?" he said. "I'll take the truck back home. You hide out here."

That wasn't what I had planned, but I liked the idea. "Okay, let's do it that way," I replied. "I'll give you ten minutes to get down the road before I call."

"Have fun," he smirked. Kissing me on the cheek, he left me alone in Dylan's enormous house. I suddenly felt like an intruder.

It was the longest ten minutes of my life. I rang his phone. "Hello, Beautiful," he said.

"I'm home," I said.

"Okay, want me to stop and bring some food to the trailer? Or did you eat?" he asked.

"I'm not at the trailer," I said.

"Where are you?" he asked.

"Your house," I replied. "Inside. Waiting on you."

"Shit! How the hell? Nevermind. I'm on my way," he said excitedly. "Nestor, hold my tab. I gotta go." I heard Nestor laughing in the background.

"Hurry home, Darlin'," I smiled as I said it.

I heard the throaty engine of the Camaro. "I can't get there fast enough."

"Don't you get a ticket," I teased.

"Levi, let you in," he said realizing how I got in the house.

"Hmm, yes. It seems like you might have mentioned that my truck already had access to your property," I pointed out.

"Grace, I had only one thing on my mind at my house the other night. You'll have to forgive me or torture me. Either way, I'm good," he laughed.

"I'm waiting," I said and hung up. I ran upstairs to the closet with clothes in it for me. Might as well go all out. I picked out a short, cute dress throwing a sweater over the top. I would have never worn such a thing just a few months ago, but things were different now. Pulling my hair back, I got shivers thinking about the nasty little peeping Dick from last night.

Running back downstairs, I heard the rumble of the garage door. I barely made it back to the living room when he came flying through the kitchen door. He stopped dead in his tracks staring at the holiday spectacle.

"Surprise," I half whimpered. By the look on his face, you would have thought I killed his best hunting dog. "It's too much. I'm sorry. I'll take it all down."

"No, don't touch it," he muttered crossing the distance between us.

"Um, okay," I hung my head.

He sat down on the couch and stared at the tree. "Sit with me," he said coaxing me next to him.

I sat down folding my legs under me. "Please don't be mad."

"Grace, I'm not mad. I'm shocked. This is more than anyone has ever done for me. I'm overwhelmed," he said.

I breathed a heavy sigh that had built up in my lungs. "You scared the shit out of me," I pouted.

"Come here," he said pulling my face to his. "You are amazing." When he released my chin, my lips practically fell on his. He pulled me closer to him as he kissed me. His warm hand trailed up my leg and over my thigh causing me to moan.

"You really do like it," I said when he allowed me to speak.

"Yes, plus the dress. Damn, I gotta have you now," he said as his eyes turned primal. I didn't need any more encouragement.

We didn't make it to the bed. I laid curled in his arms while the fire blazed and the lights twinkled. Darkness fell outside.

"Can we have Christmas here?" I asked.

"Of course, I'd love it," he said. Good grief, what took me so long to give into this man? I turned to face him, ready for round two. He recognized the glint in my eye. "Never enough."

"For you or for me?" I asked.

"Both," he laughed.

"Definitely both," I replied.

We slowly worked our way into this round, but just as things were getting hot and heavy. Both of our phones started ringing at the same time. Dylan growled and answered his. I turned mine off.

"Yeah, she's with me. He what? I swear! I'm fucking sick of trolls," Dylan shouted. "No, I'm sorry Troy. Of course, we are on our way."

"Never ending trolls. I really hope Levi is right about there being thirteen of them. Any more of them, and I'm declaring a troll war," I said.

"You need to wear something warmer," he pointed out when I grabbed the dress.

I sighed heading toward the bedroom. He followed, because everything he was wearing ended up in a heap with mine. After changing into warm fresh clothes, we drove to meet Troy.

We pulled up outside the Shady Grove Church of God in Dylan's blue truck. He was right. It was nicer than mine. It had a back-up camera and satellite radio. Several deputies stood outside along with members of the church. Dylan told me before we headed this way that we were going to the church. He knew I didn't like churches much since they tended to be so judgmental. I wasn't sure what to expect about the Church of God. I knew it was the church that Winnie loved.

Our church was branded the Baptist Church in town, but those that attended knew that it wasn't a real church. It was a portal to a thick grove of trees where our druid priest would conduct services. My kind of church.

I got out and hesitated. "Don't worry. I won't let Him strike you down," Dylan said pushing me towards the door.

"I'm not sure you are in his good graces after that little romp on the couch," I replied.

"Nothing little about that, honey," he smirked.

Men. Egos. He laughed, because I refused to acknowledge him.

"Good evening, Grace," Troy greeted me.

"Let's get on with it. How drunk is he?" I asked.

"They don't use real wine. They use grape juice," Dylan explained. I decided church was worse than I first thought. They didn't even use real wine for their communion.

I stopped at the threshold of the church as both me stared at me. "Seriously?" Dylan said already standing in the lobby.

"You never know," I replied.

"Get in here," he said waving toward the inside auditorium.

As we went in, we were greeted by the pastor of the church,

Ezekiel Stanton. Ol' Zeke had lived in Shady Grove all his life. His father was a Methodist preacher. He told me once that the CoGs as he called the Church of God, were a little livelier than the Methodist. I wasn't sure what he meant, but I nodded my head in agreement. I learned early in my life in the human realm that you don't piss off priests and preachers. They don't cast spells or hexes. They just pray to their God who in turn would destroy your life. Supposedly. I didn't take the chance.

Zeke knew what I was. I wasn't sure how knowing about fairies meshed with his religion, but he once told me that he didn't know where I fit in his faith. However, he assured me that it was on the "good side." I didn't correct him, but I was a dark fairy. Unseelie. Wild. Either way, I liked Zeke, and he liked me.

"Why Miss Grace you are looking cozy this evening. It is so good to see you in the House of God," he proclaimed.

I twisted my face at Dylan and whispered, "Is he the troll?"

"Grace," he scolded. I shrugged. You never know.

"I seem to have one of your little fellas in my communion supplies," he said. "The worst part is that he's in my office where I keep my little snack cakes. He ate them first. I love those little Christmas tree ones with the cream in the middle." Zeke had plenty of cakes in the middle. His belly bulged over his belt causing the buckle to turn downward to the earth.

"Why in the world would he want stale crackers and grape juice?" I asked.

"I didn't ask him, ma'am, but you are welcome to. He's a little too unholy for me to deal with today," he said. I had no idea what he meant as Troy led us into the back of the church behind the pulpit.

I paused for a moment feeling pressure on my head. A resistance to the room that Troy entered. Dylan grabbed my arm like he was going to force me inside, but saw my face. "What is it?"

"It's warded. I can't go in," I explained. Wards were magical force fields that kept unwanted creatures out while allowing friends to enter. Somehow the troll had gotten into the room, but I could not. I looked around the door to see if I could determine the source of the ward.

Above the door a sign proclaimed, "For a whore is a deep ditch; and a strange woman is a narrow pit."

"You've got to be kidding me," I said pointing at the sign.

Dylan chuckled. "Are you the whore or the strange woman?"

"Both," I replied.

Troy came back out. "What's the deal?"

"I can't go in. The room is warded," I said pointing at the sign. He smirked. "Shut your mouth."

"I didn't say anything," he protested. "Zeke, will you please invite Grace into your office?"

"What?" Zeke questioned.

"It's a fairy thing. Just give her permission to enter," Troy said.

"Um, okay, Miss Grace, you are welcome in my office anytime," he said leaving the door wide open for me to enter for forever. The pressure at the doorway faded and cautiously I stepped through.

A long-nosed troll lay on the floor, completely naked, staring at the ceiling fan twirling above him. "It's so pretty," he muttered.

"I thought you said the wine was fake?" I said.

"It is. I think," Dylan said.

"My Queen! It's so good to finally meet you," he said turning his eyes to me. "Whoa! How did you get to be so beautiful?"

"Jeeeeee-," I started to swear using their savior's name when Dylan covered my mouth.

"Now let's not take any chances," he said.

"Mr. Troll, are you drunk?" I asked.

He rolled over on his stomach propping his head up with his fists. "No, but I might be a bit of a glutton. Food makes me happy." A huge smile crossed his face.

"This is not your food," I said.

"Well, no, you are right. However, I saw those tasty little cakes on the preacher's desk. I ate one, then I ate them all. Then I found these stale crackers, but they taste pretty good with the juice," he explained.

"What's your name?" I asked.

"Bo," he replied.

"Just Bo?" I asked.

"That's what I said," he sassed. That's when Dylan started laugh.

Troy threw a choir robe at him. "Put that on, nasty little man."

I hissed at Dylan who continued to laugh. "If you can't control yourself, get out," I said thrusting my finger towards the door. He put his hand over his mouth as his body jerked with muffled laughter.

"Bo, get up off the floor. Troy is going to take you to your brothers," I said.

He looked at me and tiled his head. "Are you sleeping with Mr. Happy over there?" he asked pointing to Dylan who promptly stopped laughing. However, I picked up where he left off.

"That's none of your business," Dylan said.

"Oh, of course, it's not. I just wondered. Is he providing for all your needs, my Queen? I'd hate for you to have a consort who couldn't fulfill your desires," he said. I stopped laughing.

"That's enough. Out," Dylan said as he leaned to hoist the troll off the ground. The troll screeched in a high-pitched tone. We all covered our ears at the grating sound. It made my eyes water it was so loud and annoying.

"Dylan," I said calling him back. He let go.

The troll reset himself, looking at me again. "Oh, so it's a new relationship," he said.

"What the hell, Bo? This really isn't your concern," I said.

He stood up quickly. His large nose hanging over taut lips. "I beg your pardon, but it is. As your loyal subject, I must ensure that your needs are met. If he isn't doing a good enough job, I'd like to offer my services." He bowed in front of me.

I rubbed my forehead. "So, every time you try to move him, he does that?" I asked Troy.

"Yep," he said.

"Bo, would you go for a ride with me? We can discuss my relationship with Dylan more," I offered.

"Do you have cake? I'm fond of cake. It's much better than pie," Bo said.

"I disagree," Dylan muttered.

"Amen," said Zeke.

My mouth dropped at both of them. I knew what Dylan meant, but the twinge of light in Zeke's eyes led me to believe that he wasn't so innocent. A man's a man, I guessed. Holy or not.

"See, this is what is wrong with your relationship, my Queen. A real man eats cake," Bo replied. "I think it is best that I go for a ride with you. I request that he does not accompany us."

"It's my truck, buck-o," Dylan said.

"Now, Bo, if you are really concerned about my relationship, then you've got to let Dylan ride with us," I coaxed.

"But, but," he sighed. "Okay."

We loaded up in Dylan's truck. Bo sat in the back seat.

"See, this. He's driving. Is that because it makes him feel like a big man to drive and be in control?" Bo asked.

I giggled, because Dylan rolled his eyes. Big, beautiful blue eyes. "No, Bo, I drive, because she is the Queen and deserves to be chauffeured everywhere," Dylan replied.

"Dig that hole, baby," I laughed.

Bo nodded his head as if this explanation was acceptable. As we drove, we passed the speedy mart, Bo pipped up, "Oh, the store! They have the girly cakes."

"What girly cakes?" Dylan asked.

"The ones with the cute little girl on them. We must stop there," Bo said.

"No, we aren't stopping," Dylan said. Bo started the high-pitched screeching until Dylan relented.

"Are you half-Banshee?" I asked.

"No, if I were a Banshee, you would bleed out of your ears, my

Queen," he stated. I wondered if he were half-Banshee would I only bleed out of one ear.

Dylan took the troll inside, and he returned with a dozen Christmas tree cakes. "I tried to get him to get the oatmeal cream pies, but he said they were pies, not cakes."

I laughed, but I could tell that Dylan was at his final level of tolerance.

"My Queen, would you like one? I would share with you because that is what a good man would do?" Bo said.

"Do you think that Dylan doesn't share with me?" I asked.

He licked the cream off his fingers. "Well, what has he shared with you?"

His bed. His tongue. His…I was glad that didn't come out of my mouth, even though it was the first thing I thought. "I think the most important thing he shares is his time. You know, Bo that time is something we cannot get back, and we never know when it might be our last moment," I offered.

"That's a pittance when you are immortal," he scoffed. "Does he share his cakes with you?"

"I'm not really a cake kind of girl, Bo. I love sausages and meat-balls, though," I said. Dylan swerved, but righted the vehicle quickly. "He shares those with me. He even took me to the BBQ place for lunch a couple of days ago."

"It's not cake, but okay," he muttered.

"You see, Bo, we have a good relationship so far," I said.

"So far! So, you have doubts about the future! I knew it!" he latched on to nothing. It was only a few more miles to the jail.

"I have no doubts, Bo," I said as Dylan reached across to hold my hand. I laced my fingers with his. The warmth of his hand spread up my arm. Even in all the madness, he had stood by me. Steady and reliable. I had no doubts anymore.

Bo started screeching again. "Don't touch her! We are still talk-ing," he breathed between screeches. I cut my eyes to Dylan, he nodded. Pulling power from my tattoo, I turned to face the shrieking troll. I outstretched my hand, and the truck fell into silence. Granted, it was quite cold now. Bo made a beautiful ice sculpture.

"He will live," I assured Dylan.

"I know that you wouldn't kill him, Grace," he said. "No doubts? At all?"

"None," I replied.

We dropped the block of ice off at the jail which thawed as we put him in the cell. He started screeching as it melted, but ten brothers pelted him with fists until he stopped.

"Hey, Mr. Happy!" he hollered at Dylan as we walked out of holding. Dylan turned back to him. "You take care of her. She's important."

A smile spread across Dylan's face, and he bowed slightly to the troll. The rest of them waved goodbye to us as we left.

"Two more," I said.

"This is ridiculous. It was funny at first, but good fucking grief," he said.

"Vulgar mouth," I scolded him.

Fire flashed in his eyes. "Come home with me, and I'll show you how vulgar." I went home with him for the demonstration. Afterwards, I assured him that his mouth was far more vulgar than mine had ever been.

December 23rd

Dylan, Levi and I joined volunteers from the town to prepare Christmas meals for some less fortunate families in the county. Brother Rayburn coordinated our efforts. The ladies from church brought in side dishes and desserts. Brad, who seemed to weather his sausage losses, provided a semi-truck sized smoker. Dylan helped him fill it with hams and turkeys.

Kady and I packed portions into microwaveable containers, sorting them by family. Levi filled boxes, then loaded them into the back of my truck. He and Kady planned to deliver them together.

As we packed, I asked Levi, "How bad did Bethany look last night?" Levi and Winnie watched Rudolph the Red-Nosed Reindeer on television, then he went to take her home. He returned putting her in his bed.

"She is into something bad, Grace. She was out of it. She was lucid this morning, but I still didn't want to leave Winnie. I can't take the woman's child though."

"She's destroying her body. I'll ask Matthew if he knows of a rehab I can send her to get straight," I said.

Kady shook her head. "She's been to all of them. She always relapses."

I sighed. Dylan entered carrying two large hams in a foil pan. "Why the sad faces?"

"Talking about Bethany," I said.

"Levi told me she looked rough," he said. "She goes back and forth. We can invite Winnie over tomorrow night to open presents. She needs family other than her addict mother, Cletus and Tater."

"Sounds like a good plan," I responded. He winked at me as he went back outside. Levi grabbed another box and hurried out.

"Do you kiss and tell?" Kady asked.

I blushed. I don't know why, but I felt the heat rise to my face. "No," I muttered.

"Oh," she responded while dipping helpings of sweet potato casserole.

"Oh? What were you going to ask?" I prodded. Perhaps she needed reassurance that Dylan, and I were solid, and I had no designs for Levi.

"Was it good? Even after all the fake fighting," she asked boldly.

The heat intensified in my face, and I looked away.

"Oh, I see," she giggled.

"It's really none of your business," I quipped playfully.

"Don't tell Levi, but before he moved to town, I always had a crush on Dylan," she admitted. I froze in place.

"What?"

"Oh god, yes. Those blue eyes and that killer smile. I would have let him butter my biscuits anytime," she purred.

I dropped the container that had in my hand astonished that she would admit that to me. "Shit," I muttered as I bent down to clean up the mess.

She helped me. "I would never approach him now. He's yours, of course."

I didn't want to respond to her, so I just grunted something that sounded like an affirmation. Cleaning the last of the casserole off my boots, I stood. She leaned very close to me. My personal space alarm screamed in my head.

"I just always wondered if he had a big dick," she muttered as

Levi entered the room. A flash of anger washed over me, and I punched her in the face. She screamed as I lunged toward her. Levi hoisted me backwards by the waist. I struggled against him even knowing he was stronger than me.

"You, filthy whore," I spouted. She stood facing me with her hands over her nose.

"Grace, stop it," Levi begged. He put no power behind it, or I would have been subdued.

Kady began to wail. "She broke my nose."

"Dylan!" Levi screamed. "Don't make me do it, Grace."

Dylan busted through the door and muttered, "What the hell?"

Grabbing me from Levi, he dragged me out the door as I screamed profanities back at her. He pinned me to the wall by my wrists just outside the door of the community center. "Stop, now!" he ordered me.

"Don't fucking talk to me like that," I growled at him.

"Fine," he released me stepping back.

The fire rushed out of me as I listened to her pitch a hissy fit inside the building. "Shit," I mumbled leaning against the wall. "She was talking about you."

He took the step back into my personal space, but this time he leaned his forehead to mine. "Grace," he said quietly coaxing me to explain myself.

My lip quivered. I'd done the same thing he did with the peeping troll. "I'm sorry," I said.

He chuckled at me. It was like he knew. "What did she say about me?"

"She admitted to having a crush on you before Levi moved to town," I said.

"I knew that, but my heart was taken," he smiled. He didn't mean Stephanie.

"She asked if it was good. The sex."

"What did you say?" he grinned thoroughly enjoying himself. Ego much?

"I didn't answer her. I dropped a container of casserole. She helped me clean it up. When we finished, she stood almost as close as you are to me now," I said as he snaked his arm around my waist. "She wondered if…"

"If what?" he asked as he lightly kissed my neck. Brad glanced toward us, then back to his smoker.

"If it was big," I croaked.

That damn smile. "So, you defended my honor?"

"I broke her nose," I said choking back a laugh.

"My hero," he said. He kissed me softly, but pressed my body against the wall.

"Stop. Brad's watching. I've had enough voyeurs," I pleaded.

He sighed, "Okay."

I heard my truck crank up. "Where is he going?" I asked assuming it was Levi.

"Probably taking her to the med center," he said. "I'll help you pack the rest of the food." His hand found mine as we re-entered the building. Levi stood over Kady who sat in a chair with her head back. He held a hand towel over her nose.

"Who has the truck?" Levi and I said at the same time. Dylan and I rushed to the door to see a trail of dust.

"Fucking trolls!" I screamed. Dylan dialed Troy and pulled me along to his car.

"Someone just stole Grace's truck from the community center. It's full of the holiday meals for the needy," he explained. "She and I are getting in my car now to try to catch him."

We sat in the car as he revved the engine. "Gotcha. I'll let you know," he said hanging up. He flipped the phone into my lap and slammed the car into first. He shifted through the gears roughly jerking me around each time the clutch was released.

The red Camaro darted down the road following the dust trail. After several miles, I saw smoke rising over a hill. "Oh, no," I muttered.

"Could be someone burning leaves," Dylan offered.

"You know it isn't," I said. He backed off the accelerator as we created the hill. The downside was covered in small black containers, tiny shards of glass and trashed food.

My truck laid on its side. The marks on the road clearly indicated that the truck rolled several times. Sitting on the driver's side door. A thin troll sat with several containers shoveling food into his mouth.

"Can I convince you to stay in the car?" Dylan asked as he shut off the engine.

"If I get out, I'm gonna kill him," I said through gritted teeth.

"Yeah. Stay here, pretty please," he begged. I nodded and gripped my seat turning my knuckles white.

I rolled the window down so I could at least hear the conversation.

"What's your name, buddy?" Dylan asked.

The troll shoveled a large handful of ham in his mouth. Realizing it was hot, he spit it back out. "Wow! That's hot," he said.]

"Hey! I'm talking to you," Dylan said.

"Hey, Guy! I'm Ryan. Y'all have some really tasty meats in this truck. Well, it used to be a truck," he laughed.

I grabbed for the door handle, but the door locked. Dylan held the key fob in his hand. I spouted a profanity at him. "You see that Fairy Queen?" I shifted to my icy form as he stared.

"Oh! Hello my queen," he said waving.

"I'm not your fucking queen," I said punching the lock button. The door immediately locked back. I swore at Dylan again.

"She's got one hell of a vulgar mouth, but her right hook will break your nose," he explained. The troll reached up and rubbed his nose. "You are sitting on her truck."

"Oh, shit," he said, as I shot him an icy stare.

"My plan is to keep her in that car no matter how mad she gets, but you could help me out by climbing down and showing a little respect," Dylan said, locking the door again as I unlocked it.

"Sure, Guy. Glad to help. You probably won't get laid tonight," Ryan said.

Dylan looked back at me and grinned, "Sure I will." I flipped him off. Unlock. Lock.

Troy's cruiser followed by a second crested the hill, slowing to park next to the Camaro.

Unlock. Lock.

Troy heard the locks click turning to Dylan. "She's pissed," Dylan explained. I contemplated crawling out the window like the Duke boys, but I figured he'd just wrestle me to the ground. I decided to continue play with the lock just to get under his skin.

"Clearly," Troy said.

"You got this?" he asked the Sheriff.

Troy nodded. "Get her out of here," he suggested.

"Just need something out of the truck," Dylan hoisted himself up on the door. I wanted until his hand were occupied.

Unlock. Lock. "Almost, sweetheart," he laughed at me. He leaned down into the truck. Unlock. Lock. I slammed the dash with my palms.

"Ouch!" I muttered.

He raised out of the truck with my gun in hand. I kept a Kimber Pro Carry 2 in my locked glove box. Dylan had the key. I sighed as he got in the car. I'd frosted the windows with my anger built up inside the car, but with one touch of his hand, the car defrosted and my normal appearance reappeared.

"You done?" he asked.

"Yes," I muttered as I looked at the smoking remnants of my big, beautiful truck.

"When we get back to the house, I'll give you the keys to my truck," he said.

I shook my head. "No, Dylan, I can't."

"Shut your mouth," he threw at me. "I'll give you whatever I want to give you." He laughed as we pulled back up at the community center. We had a lot more packing to make up for what we lost, and I needed to apologize for hitting Kady.

"I don't like blue," I pouted.

"Fine then, walk," he teased.

"Maybe I will," I said.

He cut his eyes to me to make sure I was still joking. "I'll follow behind you just to see that ass." I slapped him hard across the arm while he laughed. He pulled up back at the community center laughing his head off.

Levi stood outside waiting for us. "Is she okay?" I asked.

"It's not broken, but I can't figure why you hit her," he said.

"She didn't tell you?" He shook his head no. "Doesn't matter. I need to apologize. Where is she?"

"Her dad took her," he said. "Where's the truck? I just want to go home."

"The troll destroyed the truck. Rolled it at least 3 times," I said.

He thought I was joking. Then it settled in on his face. "No, really?"

I sighed.

"I'm going to see what all Brad has left. See if we need to make a trip to the store. You guys pack up whatever is left in there, and I'll go get my truck," Dylan said leaving us alone.

"Levi, I'm sorry," I said.

"I just don't get it. I know that this holiday has been fucked up with this troll shit and the witches. But what is the deal with Kady? We were finally getting settled again," he whined.

I hugged him just because he needed it. He had the softest heart that I'd ever known. Everything settled in on him, and his dark brooding returned. "Levi, she started a conversation about Dylan and me that I wasn't comfortable talking about with her. She pressed it to the point where it was inappropriate," I said impressing myself with my diplomacy.

"Inappropriate? What do you mean?" he asked.

Quickly losing my pride over diplomacy, I realized I was too vague. "She asked about us, together, in the bed."

"So? Don't girls talk about that stuff?" he asked.

"Hell, if I know Dublin? It's not like I've got a ton of girl-friends," I said. "I avoided her direct questions until she told me that she once had a crush on him before you moved to town. She asked about the sex and if it was good. Then she proceeded to ask about the size of…"

"La, la, la, la, la," he said sticking his fingers in his ears. "No more! No more!

I laughed at him. "I still shouldn't have hit her," I said. He dialed a number on his phone and handed it to me.

"Levi, you tell that wench that I'm going to kick her ass the next time I see her. You move out of that trailer right now. She's nothing but trash," she said without saying hello.

"I'm sorry I hit you, Kady," I said.

"Grace?"

"Here's Levi," I said shoving the phone back at him. "I said it. I won't say it again. If you want to move, be my guest." I stomped off into the community center. It was quiet. All the other volunteers had left, and the rest of the food was gone. Dylan entered the backdoor.

"Brad is gone too," he said. "Is that weird?"

Cocking my head sideways at him, I said, "Do you really have to ask that in this town?"

"I want to go home," he said.

"I want to go with you," I said.

"Well, then, let's go."

We called Nestor to take Levi home, but he begged all of us to come the bar for coffee. The soul healing kind. Reluctantly, we agreed. We sat on three stools at the bar. There were a few patrons there watching television and playing pool. I sipped my coffee while next to me Dylan rested a warm hand on my thigh. On his opposite side, the dark-eyed bard brooded. Kady had blessed him out for calling her and passing me the phone.

"I can't believe she asked you that," he muttered finally. It was the first thing he'd said to me since he handed me the phone back at the community center. He took a long sip of his coffee, staring into the cup.

Remaining silent, Dylan wrapped his arm around my waist almost pulling me off the stool, but somehow, he managed to steady me and not let go. "Levi, I've known for years that she had a crush on me, but she's with you. Who cares what she asked Grace? Maybe she was just trying to be friendly after everything that has happened," Dylan offered.

"Actually, I thought she was trying to make sure that I didn't like Levi," I admitted. "I really am sorry."

"Stop apologizing. There is nothing you can do about it. Now the truck is trashed, and we've still got to survive one more troll," Levi slipped into deep brood mode.

"She is going to take my truck, because I said so. Plus, it's just one more," Dylan said.

"And their mother is coming to town. She's probably fantastic," I poured on the sarcasm.

We all took sips of the coffee. Nestor went ahead and topped off each cup. Dylan dumped his regular two scoops of sugar in his, stirring it with a spoon. The bar door whooshed open behind us. I swore it was getting colder by the minute outside. Kady strode in with her hands on her hips. Her face was partially covered by a puffy coat hood with fur around the edges.

"Levi Rearden, why aren't you answering your phone?" she yelled.

Levi dropped his head so hard it hit the bar. He proceeded to knock it on the bar multiple times.

"Miss Rayburn, this is a business. Please keep your voice down, and for heaven's sake, shut the damn door," Nestor said.

"Yes, sir," she mumbled closing the door.

Dylan let go of my waist and pulled me from the stool to sit at a table. The table from the night we played pool. "Let them talk," he muttered. "But surely Levi could do better. She's a little unstable."

"His first girlfriend was a voodoo priestess. I thought he *was* doing better," I replied.

"Point made," he said pulling my chair right next to him. "You are too far away."

Leaning over, I put my head on his shoulder as he wrapped his arm around my shoulders. We watched Levi and Kady talk at the bar. Surprisingly, I couldn't hear a word they were saying. Levi refused to look at her, either staring at his coffee or up at the television above the bar.

"If the truck wasn't wrecked, I'd say let's just leave them, but I hate to leave him behind. Especially if they fight," I said.

We sat and watched them talk. Eventually, Kady left Levi sitting alone at the bar. My heart broke for him. He was too good to have to put up with a crazy woman. Other than me, of course. Standing from the chair, I grabbed our empty cups. Dylan let me get up and talk to him without saying a word.

I sat the cups on the bar. "More?" Nestor asked.

"No. Thank you, Nestor," I said. Even though he was my grandfather, I still hadn't gotten to the point where I called him anything other than his real name.

"I suppose we are done," Levi said with red eyes. Lord have mercy. If that woman made him cry, I was going to do more than break her nose.

Putting my hand on his chin, I lifted his face to look at me. "She's not worth it, Dublin. I know your heart desperately is looking for a home. It's your nature. One day you will find it. I promise. Despite anything she's done to me, I never wanted to see your heart break."

He swallowed, "Grace, I just want to go home."

"Alright. I'm going to stay here at the bar, and Dylan is going to take you back home," I said.

"I'll walk. I need the fresh air," he said.

"Levi, it's colder than a witch's tit in a brass bra. Let Dylan take you home," I said.

"No," he said. "Thanks, Nestor." He kissed me on the forehead and went out into the cold.

13

CHRISTMAS EVE

SITTING AT THE BAR IN DYLAN'S BEAUTIFUL HOUSE, I STARED OUT
the windows while sipping my coffee. I'd skipped the sugar. I'd
rather taste it on his lips. He went for a jog. As I bided my time, my
imagination went wild thinking about a hot and sweaty Mr. Sandy
Hair returning. I'd had more sex in the last couple of days than I'd
had the entire time I'd agreed to the contract with the Sanhedrin. I
was nowhere near satisfied. Thankfully, he showed no signs of
stopping either.

Dylan technically wasn't a fairy, but you would have never
known with the libido. Last night as we laid in bed discussing the
havoc over the last few days, he mentioned that he too started off
with restrictions on a contract with the Sanhedrin. Once they realized he was different that most immortals, they released him to do
as he wished.

That's when he met Stephanie. Or rather, when she threw
herself at him one night at The Hot Tin Roof Bar. Dylan and Levi
had something in common. They weren't the one-night stand kind
of guys. Over the years, Stephanie and Dylan kept up a relationship, but the entire time, she slept with whoever she wanted. He
didn't talk much about it, but I felt I should reciprocate his story.

I told him about meeting Remington Blake in a bar on the
other side of Tuscaloosa. He teased me for not sleeping with Remy
as soon as I met him. I think I didn't, not only because of Jeremiah

and the Sanhedrin, but because part of me knew Remy wasn't completely truthful with me. My hormones were louder than my instinct though. The sex with Remy was great. I didn't think he was sleeping with anyone else, not even his wife. I'm not entirely sure, but if had just been up front with me, I probably would have slept with him anyway, because he was a fairy. His lie to me was the closest I'd ever come to having a broken heart.

None of it mattered now. I had Dylan, and I loved him. There were moments like yesterday when I punched Kady that I wondered if he regretted his decision to commit himself to a wild fairy like myself. I frequently had problems controlling my feelings. Well, anger mostly. Okay, anger only, but still, I would have to make an effort to calm myself for his sake.

"Grace! Hey, Grace," his voice brought me back from my thoughts. There he stood at the back door with a microfiber, athletic towel drying his face. The sun from the kitchen window glinted off his sweaty skin. My hormones went into overdrive.

"Hey, I want you right now," I said.

Shock registered on his face, but then he grinned. "Insatiable," he said. "One day I won't be enough for you."

"Never," I said, washing my coffee cup out.

"I'm sweaty and need a shower," he protested as I stalked toward him. It just turned me on more that he was making excuses.

"I don't give a flying fuck," I said.

He took off running up the steps toward the bedroom, and I chased him. He was much faster than me. He was in the bathroom completely stripped, turning on the shower water when I walked in. I dropped the robe I was wearing on the floor. He pulled me into the shower with him.

"Do you have a housekeeper?" I asked him after our shower. I'd noticed last night that all the candles he had in the room were gone.

He rubbed a towel through his hair while he picked through his closet. I'd already picked out clothes to wear, so I'd managed to get dressed before he did. "No, why do you ask?"

"What did you do with all the candles?"

"You cleaned them up, right?" he said.

"Um, no," I replied. "I've been with you except when I was with Levi the other day shopping and putting up the tree downstairs."

He stared at the room, but turned back to his closet. He pulled out a brown button up shirt, throwing it on the bed with a pair of jeans. "Are you teasing me?" he finally said.

"Darlin' I'm serious. I didn't do anything with the candles," I said.

He growled. "I need a better security system apparently," he replied.

"That's creepy," I said.

"Probably some fucking troll," he said frustrated.

"I'm sorry," I said dipping my head.

He placed his warm hands on my cheeks and kissed my forehead. "It's not your fault."

"If I hadn't decided to do this Queen thing, this town might be normal," I said.

"This town was never normal, Grace," he replied pulling on his jeans. He picked up the shirt as I slipped off the bed. I moved his hands kissing his chest before I buttoned up his shirt for him.

Just as I started to kiss him, his phone rang. "Ugh," he groaned and answered, "Riggs."

On the other side, I could hear someone frantically talking. "Okay, we are on the way," he said as his face turned grave.

"What is it?" I asked before he hung up.

He grabbed his leather jacket and tossed it to me. I drank in the smell. "We have to get to the med center," he said. "That was Dr. Mistborne. They brought Bethany in. She's unresponsive."

"Shit," I said grabbing his phone. I'd left mine downstairs.

"It's okay. Levi has Winnie. He's the one that found her," he said grabbing my hand as we left the bedroom. "We will meet him down at the med center."

We took his truck. He drove like a maniac. "Would you slow down?"

"I'm trained to drive like this. You have to do it for the Sheriff's Department," he said.

I knew he was elected Sheriff, but that the Sanhedrin basically insured that he would win no matter what. According to state law, he had to complete regular law enforcement standards before taking the job. He'd had no issues completing all their tests. Still, I gripped the arm rest with white knuckles for the ten-minute drive into town.

We pulled up outside the emergency room and rushed in. Dr. Mistborne waited for us at reception. "The doctors are working on her. She's breathing now, but we don't know how long she was unconscious," Tabitha explained.

"Why aren't you working on her?" I asked.

"She's not a fairy. She is in good hands, Grace. I put Levi and Winnie in a private waiting room. Come with me," she said. When we reached the room, she nodded to us both leaving us to enter alone.

Levi sat in one of the chairs with Winnie wrapped around his neck. Kady sat next to him and stroked her hair. She looked up when we entered the room. Her sweet little eyes were red and bloodshot. No child should ever cry on Christmas Eve. At that moment, I hated Bethany Jones for what she was doing to this lovely child. Winne jumped from Levi's lap, running toward me. I bent down to meet her as she buried her head in my neck.

"Mommy was cold and wouldn't wake up," she said. My heart shattered into a million pieces. "Uncle Levi called the doctors for her."

Dylan wiped a tear from his eye while he kept his hand on my back. He pushed a little guiding me to one of the chairs. I sat down and held her.

"I'll be right back," he said. "Levi, come here."

Levi looked puzzled as they exited the room. Kady didn't look at me. Her face was slightly purpled and her eyes were red. "I can heal it, Kady," I said to her.

She shot a look at me. At first, I thought it was defiance, but it quickly faded to regret. She was sorry she said the things she'd said to me. Even if it were only for Levi's sake, I'd forgive her.

"Just take care of Winnie. I'm okay," she said.

I patted the seat next to me. She reluctantly got up sitting down next to me cautiously. "We can't fight. Next to Dylan and this little angel, Levi means the world to me. He's my family. I want him happy, and if you are that happy, then I'm fine with his decision. Please let me heal it."

She nodded, and I lifted my hand to her face. Pulling power from my tattoo, I pushed a warm healing into her face as tears rolled down her cheeks. The bruising faded, but the red eyes stayed. There wasn't anything more I could do about that than I could about my own red eyes.

"Thank you, Grace. I didn't deserve that. What I said about liking Dylan was true, but I said it to provoke you. Levi loves you, and I just wanted him to see you for who you really are. I was wrong," she said.

"I love Levi, but I don't think it's what you think," I said.

She shook her head a little. "I think if Dylan hadn't come back that he wouldn't have bothered with me."

"I know that if Dylan hadn't come back, I'd be too devastated to have a relationship with anyone. Not to mention, Levi is totally the settle down and have a family type of guy. Until Dylan, I never imagined that for myself. Not even with Levi. I'll admit when he walks across my living room without his shirt on or when he blushes, my hormones go wild." She giggled, because she completely understood. "But I would have never made a move on him."

"Why?" she asked.

I paused for a moment. My reason was because my heart belonged to Dylan whether he was dead or alive. If Dylan hadn't come back, would I have considered Levi? I knew the answer was that I'd probably fucked him, ruined his life, and sent him packing. Searching deeper though, I knew the reason I wouldn't have made a move on Levi was because he still had a lot to learn about life. Sex between us would have been amazing, however he would want more. I'd never given more. "Because once wouldn't have been enough for him. I cared about him too much for me to ruin him."

I'd just admitted to her that I was a whore, but it didn't matter. She seemed to understand. "How do you know if you are in love?" she asked me.

"I'm not an expert in that department. Levi actually told me many times that I was in love with Dylan, but I refused to admit it. So, I can't answer that question for you. However, I beg of you to decide what you want from Levi and be honest. He's tender hearted. I'll be there to pick up whatever broken pieces he has, but I'd rather not have to do that," I answered.

"He's said that he loves me, but I haven't said it back. You are right. I should be honest and tell him that I'm not sure, but that I want him to give me time to figure it out," she said as Levi and Dylan came back into the room. The stared at us sitting next to each other. Winnie quietly snoozed on my shoulder.

"Your nose," Levi said.

Kady nodded her head toward me. He smiled beckoning her to him. Wrapping his arms around her, he kissed her lightly as Dylan sat next to me. I tore my eyes from them. If she did anything to hurt my bard, I'd rip her nose off. Taking a deep breath, I looked toward Dylan. Winnie stirred.

"Winnie, let's go see if they have some grits in the cafeteria," Levi said.

"What about mommy?" she asked still half-asleep.

"We will check on her after we eat. The doctors are taking care of her," he said. She slipped from my arms and took Levi's hand.

The door to the private waiting room clicked shut as Dylan ran his hand into mine. Folding his strong fingers around mine, he said, "She's not doing good. Winnie showed up at your house this morning and told Levi that her mom wouldn't wake up. He left her with Kady to run and check on Bethany. She wasn't breathing. He performed CPR on her until the paramedics arrived. They shocked her back, but he said it was at least ten minutes before they got there. We need to face the fact that she's probably gone. The doctors won't give me any firm information. I called Blake. He's on the way."

"You called Remy?" I asked.

"Yes, he has the paperwork saying that you are her guardian if something happens, right?" he asked.

"Yes, but Bethany is still alive," I offered.

"Even if she survives this, I doubt she will be able to take care of Winnie for a long time. Hopefully the paperwork is in order because we don't want to have to fight the state over custody. I called Troy, too. He's on the way to get copies of the paperwork," he said.

I stood and paced the room. Either temporarily or permanently, I was about to become a mother. It terrified me. I was not mother material. "I'm not sure I can do this," I muttered.

He stopped my pacing by putting his arms round me. "I'll do it with you. You love her. You've fed and clothed her since you moved into the trailer park. There are no less than twenty presents under my tree for her. There is a stocking hanging from my mantle for her. There is a room upstairs that is all hers. We can do this."

My heart pounded because I couldn't accept that this wonderful man was mine. "I'm sorry," I muttered.

"For what?"

164

"Waiting so long to tell you that I loved you," I said. "I'm a big sappy fool now. Look at me."

"You look amazing. Besides, I knew," he said.

"Oh really? So sure, about yourself, huh?" I teased.

"No, just sure about us," he replied. Tabitha walked in smiling at us.

"Have they told you anything?" she asked.

"No, I have rights to Winnie. Remy is coming with the paperwork, but I've got nothing that says I can know her medical information," I replied.

She grimaced. "I can't tell you then, but it's not good. I'm glad you have paperwork for Winnie. You are going to need it." She turned and walked out. She'd told us everything we needed to know without saying anything at all. I liked her. We needed to have lunch together sometime soon.

"You still want everyone to come to my house tonight?" Dylan asked.

"Yes, I think we definitely need it now. Besides, we already invited everyone," I said. "Winnie will love the room. Maybe it will help her cope with Bethany."

"Did you invite Kady?" he asked.

I smiled, "I forgot, but she should be there too. We talked a little. I think it all stemmed from her doubts about my feelings for Levi."

"I figured as much. Still, I can't believe she pushed it as far as she did. To be honest, I hope they don't work out," he said.

"Dylan! That's terrible," I said.

He laughed. "Is it? She's immature for a woman in her mid-twenties," he said.

"I'd say she's just a mature as I'd expect her to be," I replied.

"Maybe so," he said. There was a light knock on the door. Dylan released me. "Come in."

In an expensive suit, former state prosecutor, Remington Blake entered the room with a briefcase. His face was pale. "Morning," he said simply.

"What's wrong, Remy?" I asked.

"I just talked to the doctors, because I had the custody papers for Winnie, so they told me her status," he said.

"We know it's bad," I said.

He shook his head. "No child should lose a parent at Christmas," he muttered.

"She's gone?" I choked out as Dylan put an arm around my waist.

"No, she's brain dead. Her body is still alive. She has no will, so they will keep her hooked up until a relative makes the call or her body gives up. I know her mother isn't capable of doing it. I feel bad that she's going to sit there in that bed like that," he sounded genuinely sad. I'd known Remy for a long time, but I'd never known him to soft-hearted. It was a side he never showed me. He was always playful and seductive. "The paperwork will allow you to take her even though she's still alive. It wasn't dependent upon her death."

I breathed a sigh of relief because I wouldn't have to fight for her. If it had come to that, I would have though.

Hearing a commotion in the hallway, Dylan moved quickly to the door. His instincts were always to run toward the fire, not away from it. "You fools, pipe down," he yelled.

"Hey, look its Sheriff Riggs," I heard Cletus say.

In an instant Cletus and Tater joined us in the waiting room, they both looked grave. "Where is Bethany?" Tater asked.

"She's with the doctors. She's not doing good," I replied.

"What about Winnie?" Cletus asked.

"She's getting some breakfast in the cafeteria with Levi," I replied.

They both hung their heads. Tater always wore a trucker hat, but he removed it revealing a large bald spot that shined under the fluorescent lights. "She's been in some bad stuff," Tater muttered.

"Drugs?" I asked.

"Yeah, we told her to stop, but she never paid any attention to us," Cletus said.

Cletus and Tater were idiots, but I'd never known either of them to do drugs. "She's gonna die?" Tater asked as tears welled up in his eyes. I could only nod in response.

"You will take Winnie, right?" Cletus asked.

"I still have the paperwork. I think the only person that could take her away from me would be her father, whoever he is," I said.

"He ain't around no more," Tater said. "He was a dealer. I saw on the news a few years ago that he was killed in a shootout in Birmingham."

Poor Winnie. Drug dealer father. Addict mother. Heart of gold. I'd do everything I could to make sure that she got everything she deserved and so much love.

"Will you guys get to stay in her trailer?" I asked.

They looked at each other than at me. "Miss Grace, the trailer is ours. Tater's daddy gave it to us when he died. We let Bethany live there so Winnie would have a roof over her head," Cletus explained. My heart exploded. All these years I thought it was Bethany who let them live there. I rushed across the room and hugged them both.

"We came down to make sure you had Winnie," Tater said.

"Thank you, both. She will be loved," I said.

"I ain't got no doubt about that," Cletus said. "You can send Levi over to get her stuff. We will put it in some boxes for you. I just picked some up at the liquor store. They have the best boxes."

Child's toys and clothes in liquor boxes. Only in Shady Grove, Alabama. "Thanks, guys."

They slipped out of the room as Remy laid papers out on a side table. "I need you to sign a few things, Grace."

I looked over the papers. They were just confirmations that I was taking her with me per the previous contract signed by her mother. As I signed each one as Remy indicated, Nestor and Mable showed up speaking to Dylan quietly. When I finished, I handed them all to Remy. "What's next?" I asked.

"That's it. You are a mother," he said. "You will do a great job. Don't doubt yourself." He smiled and patted Dylan on the shoulder as he left the room.

I jumped up hugging Nestor. He rocked side to side with me. "He's right. You are going to be a great mother," he said.

After Remy squared the paperwork with Troy, Dylan and I took Winnie back to the trailer. Levi went across the street, retrieving the boxes from Cletus and Tater. It was a shame that the entirety of what she owned fit into two boxes. She was very quiet after we explained that she would come and live with us until her mother got better. She even asked me if her mother was going to die. I told her that I didn't know, but that I knew her mother loved her very much which was probably the biggest lie I'd ever told. Bethany was selfish. The drugs and prostitution were a never-ending cycle. She'd dragged Winnie through it for six years. Part of me was glad that Winnie would have a home where she was loved and cared for every single day. The other part of me was terrified that I couldn't live up to what she needed.

She sat on the couch with Rufus curled up in her lap. She stroked him lightly while watching cartoons. I packed a bag for her and myself to take to Dylan's for the night. Levi and Kady went to the diner for lunch, but I wasn't hungry. Dylan made peanut butter sandwiches, but Winnie barely touched hers.

"You just about ready?" Dylan asked.

"Almost. A couple more things. Then I've got cooking to do for dinner tonight," I said. "Winnie, we are going to Mr. Dylan's house for dinner and open some presents. You want to help me cook?"

Her eyes twinkled for a minute, then she nodded. "Can we make cookies again?"

"Absolutely!" I replied.

Standing in Dylan's kitchen with Winnie on a stool next to me decorating cookies, Nestor and Mable arrived. She gushed over the house and the decorations. "I swear. It looks like a real home, Dylan. It's lovely."

"Thanks, Miss Mable. I blame Grace for the decorations," he said smiling.

"Blame!" I exclaimed.

"You did it didn't you?" he teased.

"Well, yes," I said. "I guess it is my fault."

They laughed as they followed Dylan to the other rooms while he gave them the grand tour. Levi arrived with Kady. They had been to the store and picked up a few last-minute items for cooking. Levi immediately started helping Winnie finish off the cookies. Kady stared at the living room and the decorations. "It's beautiful," she said.

"Thanks," I replied.

She joined Winnie and Levi. Rufus ran around my feet. We couldn't leave the mutt back at the house, so he was here, too, with his own stocking hanging by the fireplace. I caught up with Dylan's tour as he opened the door to Winnie's room. We hadn't showed it to her yet.

"Dylan, this is amazing," Mable cooed. "You will make a great Daddy."

"Um, well, I'm not exactly directly involved with that. She still calls me Mr. Dylan," he stumbled over his words.

"Don't let him fool you. He will be a great Daddy," I said behind them. A blush crossed his cheeks. "Dinner is ready if you guys are hungry."

"I'm starving," Nestor exclaimed. He'd closed the Hot Tin Roof Bar for the first time on Christmas Eve. The sign on the bar said, "Closed for Christmas. Happy Holidays from the Gwinn family."

I stood in Winnie's room alone with Dylan. "I've never had a family to celebrate Christmas," he said softly.

"Me either," I replied. "I used to take presents to Winnie, but never got to see her open them. Generally, I spent time home alone watching the parades on television while killing a bottle of Crown."

"Stephanie never invited me to her family Christmas. She said her mother didn't approve of us living together without being married," he said.

"What? Her mother is Elvish right? They don't traditionally get married. They mate for life," I said.

"I just went by what she said," he muttered.

I hugged him drinking in the scent of musk and peppermint. "No more," I said.

After dinner, we opened presents. Winnie squealed with all the toys that she got. "I'm taking them home to your house Aunt Grace," she exclaimed.

"I have a gift for you, Winnie," Dylan said.

"Oh really?" she jumped and clapped. Tonight was really about her. She brought the wonder and life of a child to our celebration.

"Yep, come with me," he said holding his hand out to her. She put her small hand in his strong one looking up at him adoringly. We followed them up the stairs. He opened the door to the play-room, and she stood stunned.

"You've got to be kidding me," she exclaimed. I laughed at her sassy remark.

"All yours. You can come and play anytime you want," he said. She wrapped her arms around his legs squeezing him. A tear appeared in the corner of his eye as he scooped her up. She giggled and hugged him.

"Uncle Levi, go get my toys!" she ordered.

"Please," I prompted.

"Puleeze!" she added.

He laughed but headed downstairs to grab the oodles of toys and clothes she'd gotten. He returned arms full. She instructed him where to put everything. We let her enjoy it.

"Okay, we need to open the adult's presents," I said.

She clapped excited for everyone else. "And eat cookies?" she asked.

"Sure," I replied. She took off down the stairs in a dead sprint. My heart cringed as she hit the top step. Visions of her tumbling down the steps flowed through my mind. "Slow down, little lady," I called to her trying to mask my concern.

"Yes ma'am," she said as she slowed down.

Dylan wrapped me up from behind. "See, you're already doing mommy things," he whispered in my ear.

"Christmas is all about the truest gifts in our life. She is one amazing little gift," I replied.

We joined them in the living room as the fire blazed. Everyone had exchanged gifts, except for the gift I got Levi. Dylan wanted us to wait until Christmas morning to open presents. Levi played Christmas songs on his guitar. I took in the scene. My family. I loved them all. I never dreamed of my heart being so full. Winnie would have another round of Santa's gifts in the morning.

"Levi, here you go," I said handing him a small box.

"Glad you went all out," he smirked at the size of the box. He ripped off the meager wrapping and pulled out a black key on a basic keychain. His eyes widened. "What's the key go to?"

"It's in the garage," I said. He jumped up and tore through the kitchen faster than a hot knife through butter. Dylan, Kady and I followed him closely. Beside Dylan's Camaro, a new Harley

Davidson Softail Breakout sat with a denim blue paint job to match his eyes. He stood in shock. "You okay, Dublin?"

"Damn, Grace. It's a beauty. It's brand, spankin' new!" he gushed.

"I'm tired of you borrowing my truck. The truck I don't have anymore. Now we gotta share the Harley," I joked. I thought he'd crank it up immediately, but he rushed across the room wrapping his arms around me.

"That's better than the sweater I got you," he muttered in my ear.

"Don't be silly. I love my sweater," I said. As he squeezed me tight, his fingers brushed under the edges of my shirt. I felt that familiar fairy tingle. He did too because he froze in place and backed away.

"Sorry," he blushed. Hot damn, that boy.

"What?" Dylan said.

"Tell you later," I said. "There are helmets there on the shelf." As much as it pained me, I bought two helmets. I figured Kady would need one too.

"For me?" she asked. I nodded. They donned the helmets as Dylan opened the garage door. He fired up the engine. It rumbled in the garage shaking the walls with the power. I'd had the dealership deliver it, so I hadn't actually heard it run.

"Wow," I said. "Don't kill yourself!" I shouted at him. He grinned.

Right after Dublin came to live with me, he told me that he'd left a rebuilt motorcycle behind at his dad's house. I made the effort to retrieve the motorcycle for him, only to find out that his drunken father sold it for booze money. I didn't have the heart to tell him, so I'd intended to buy him a new one for Christmas. By the look on his face, he loved it. Kady saddled up behind him, then they tore off down the drive.

"You left the gate open?" I asked Dylan.

"Yep," he smiled. "What was that look there between the two of you?"

"You jealous?" I asked.

"No, but you did say you'd tell me," he said.

"When fairies touch, there's a tingle. Just so happens that the tingle in strong between us. Probably because I claimed him. Either way, it catches us off-guard sometimes," I explained trying to make it sound as innocent as possible.

"He can never touch you again," Dylan proclaimed.

"I'm okay with that," I shrugged.

"No swapping gravy," he said.

"The magical kind or the sexy kind?" I asked.

"Both!" he exclaimed.

"You are cramping my style, Dylan Riggs," I said.

He shot me a look. "Feel free to leave."

"I can't. I don't have a vehicle," I said.

"Guess you will just have to abide by the rules," he said.

I sighed, but smiled at him. He didn't want me touching Levi, but he joked around with it. I'd reassure him later that I only wanted to touch him.

We went back inside. Winnie was getting sleepy. "Okay little girl! Santa doesn't come if you are awake. You can sleep in your new room."

"We have to leave cookies and milk!" she said. "I never get to leave them, because mommy never has cookies!"

I helped her make a plate of cookies. We placed them on the hearth near the fireplace. Dylan and I tucked her in bed. As he read "The Night Before Christmas," her eyelids drooped. We kissed her goodnight and turned on a nightlight that shined stars on the ceiling. She slept before we shut the door.

I went back downstairs to see Nestor stealing kisses from Mable. "Hey, hey, none of that, I protested."

Miss Mable blushed. "You don't hold back," Nestor said indicating Dylan. He had a point.

"Your cell phone rang, Dylan," Mable said.

"Troll," I muttered.

Dylan redialed the last number. It was Levi. He listened to Levi talk, and his face turned darker than I'd ever seen it. "Okay, we will be there in a few minutes," he said.

"Where are we going?" I asked knowing it was a troll.

"Your trailer," he muttered as he took my hand. "We will be back. Please listen for Winnie."

"We've got her. Go ahead," Nestor said.

We loaded up in his truck. His demeanor scared me. Something was very, very wrong. "Dylan, what did Levi say?"

"I'm not sure I believe it. Let's just get there," he said grabbing my hand. He squeezed hard.

As we approached the trailer park, two fire engines and two sheriff's cruisers sat with flashing lights. For all the vehicles, I couldn't see the trailer, but smoke wafted through the air.

"Oh, no," I muttered.

Dylan squeezed my hand again as he parked behind the vehicles. Troy and Levi waited on us. "How bad?" Dylan asked.

Troy just shook his head. I pushed past them as the fire fighters sprayed water toward my trailer. When I finally cleared the trucks, I stopped dead in my tracks. The smoking carcass of the double wide sat in the darkness. Somewhere behind me, I heard Dylan's voice. Covering my mouth with my hands, I stood in shock as my home was utterly destroyed. Dylan's body hit mine with a thud as he wrapped his arms around me just before my knees buckled. His body slowly guided mine to the wet grass.

I shook in shock, anger and a thousand other emotions that rolled over me. "It's okay, Grace. It's going to be okay," he spoke softly in my ear.

"What the hell?" I muttered. Levi walked up standing next to us. Kady leaned into him as we watched the embers smolder. "Where is it?"

"Where is what?"

"The fucking troll!" I said as anger washed over me. The glamour dropped. My tattoo flared to life as the filigree stretched under my shirt and across my chest. The faint glow of power could be seen through my long sleeves. Dylan held tight to me. Usually his warmth and power kept me from turning, but the fire in me burned ice cold. With one swift motion, I broke his hold standing to my feet. I twirled as the silvery dress flowed around my ankles.

He stood up before me. "Grace, you've got to calm down."

"My fucking house is gone! These ridiculous morons have destroyed my town, my truck and now my HOME!" I screamed. "Move!"

He stepped aside letting me pass. "I'm your home," he muttered as I passed. The cold rushed out of me to spread out across the ground causing an instant frost. The firefighters stared at me as their hoses turned to ice. The remaining heat in the trailer frosted over. The tattoo faded, and my normal appearance returned.

Stepping in front of me again, he brushed my tears away. "Everything that is important to you is still here. Winnie. Levi. Nestor. The town."

"You," I muttered.

"Yeah," he replied placing a soft kiss on my lips.

Troy approached cautiously. "He's in the cruiser over here if you want to talk to him."

"I probably shouldn't," I said.

"He filled the trailer full of candles and waited for you to come home. He had it in his head that he wanted to marry you. I'm not really clear on how he got the idea, but he said that he knew you liked rooms full of candles," Troy said.

It was either laugh or cry. So, I laughed. For a moment, I was sure Dylan thought I'd gone mad, but I heard Levi chuckling behind me. Levi had seen the room full of candles when he helped me decorate the tree.

"I guess we know who cleaned up the bedroom," Dylan said, then he started laughing.

A muffled banging came from the parked cruiser. I could see a man inside banging on the window. "Let me talk to him," I said.

"You sure?" Dylan asked. I nodded.

Troy opened the back door of the cruiser. This troll was different that the others. He had smooth, young skin. A smile crossed his lips, and he blushed as I looked at him. His green eyes twinkled. He actually would have been very attractive had he not burned my home to the ground.

"What's your name?" I asked.

"Taylor," he muttered.

"Taylor, what were you doing in my house?"

"I wanted to surprise you, my Queen. You deserve a good mate, and I think I'm the best man you could ever have," he explained. "I wanted to propose to you on Christmas Eve, so I collected the candles and lit them all. Only I think I got one too close to a curtain or something. Before I knew it, the whole thing was on fire." He hung his head in shame.

"First of all, you see this man right here?" I asked pointing toward Dylan. Taylor lifted his eyes to look at Dylan. "He's my everything. I'll respectfully decline your proposal. You will go and sit with your brothers in jail."

"I'm so sorry, beautiful Grace," he said. For a moment, his voice sounded just like Dylan's. We looked at each other and shrugged. Only Dylan addressed me like that.

"Taylor, how did you know to say that?" I asked.

"My brother, Richard, likes to spy on things. I had him watching you ever since I saw you on television. I knew that you didn't kill those children. I fell in love. My mother is going to be so disappointed because I told her I was getting married."

"You did things a little out of order," I said.

"Actually, Lamar said that courting women is like tipping cows. Sometimes you have to give them a little poke before they fall for you," he said.

Levi snorted, and Kady slapped him on the arm. Then I wondered if all of this didn't center around Taylor. "Did all of your brothers help you with this?"

"Yes, they did! My brothers are great. Phil, Willie, Kevin, Ryan and Phillip were in charge of the reception food. Eric was making us some rings from some spare metal he found. Cory and his wife were making a wedding stew. Bo was in charge of the cake. He insisted that it be a Christmas tree cake. He's obsessed with them. Chad collected bowls for us to put the stew and other goodies in," he said.

"What about Keith? Mr. Anger Management," I asked puzzled as to what his role was in the whole plan.

"Oh, nothing. He was mad that I'd claimed you. I think he wanted you for himself," he admitted. "But I knew you were mine from the moment I saw you."

"Taylor, you realize we aren't getting married, right?" Somewhere in all of this I managed a little compassion.

He nodded, but looked defeated. "We only have one problem."

"Yeah, what's that?"

"Mother," he said. "She's going to kill me for getting her to come to Alabama for the wedding, and then there isn't going to be a wedding."

"As a being from the Otherworld, I can protect you if you request it," I offered. Dylan shook his head next to me. I knew what he'd say. How could I pick and choose who I protected? I supposed burning down my home might factor in at some point.

"Yes, please," he said.

"Okay, Troy, take him to the jail. I know you are full, but hopefully this will all be over once their mother shows up," I said. "Go home and enjoy Christmas with Amanda and Mark."

"I plan on it. Santa Claus is coming!" he smiled. "How's Winnie?"

"Distracted at the moment," I said.

"Good. See you tomorrow," he said climbing into the cruiser. Poor Taylor waved at me sadly.

"I'm taking Kady home," Levi said. "I guess you are staying at Dylan's house?"

"You all are," Dylan said. "There is plenty of room."

Levi hopped on the Harley and Kady wrapped herself around him. I turned to Dylan because I knew he had something to say about my offer of protection. "Spit out, Dylan Riggs," I prodded.

"He burned your house down!" he exclaimed.

"All I saw was a young, sad troll who wanted to impress a girl. He fucked up. We've all fucked up before, right?" I asked.

"Yes," he muttered.

"Has the great Dylan Riggs ever fucked up?" I teased.

He shook his head, "You know I have."

"Say something sweet. Lay it on me," I continued to press. He wouldn't smile, damnit.

He shook his head as he turned to head toward the truck. "Let's go home," he said.

"Aw, come on, Dylan," I pleaded. He held the door open for me as I climbed in. He paced around the truck, but didn't speak once he got in. He didn't speak the whole way back to his place.

We pulled into the garage. He turned off the truck, but just sat there. The motorcycle sat in the corner, so I knew Levi had returned. I supposed he didn't spend much time with Kady after he left the trailer park.

Finally, Dylan spoke, "I fucked up by waiting too long to go after you," he said.

"It worked out," I smiled.

"Yes," he muttered. I slipped across the seat, threw my leg over his and tucked myself between him and the steering wheel. He shifted his weight below me. "What are you doing, Grace?"

"Making up for lost time," I smiled. Finally, a smile flirted with the edges of his lips. I leaned over and kissed the edges of his mouth. With each kiss, the smile grew. Placing my palm on the window, the windows in the truck frosted over.

"You could still marry the troll," he teased.

"I have everything thing I never dreamed of right here," I said.

"Never dreamed?"

"Never in a million years," I replied.

We steamed up the cab enough the windows eventually defrosted. When we entered the living room, Nestor sat on the couch waiting for us. His concerned eyes met me as I straightened my clothes. He smiled knowing we'd been home for over an hour.

"Everything okay?" he asked.

"The trailer is gone," I said.

"What?"

"Burned to a husk, fucking trolls," I said.

Nestor looked worried. "You can stay in the apartment above the bar," he offered. Bless him.

"Um, no, she's staying here," Dylan said.

"I didn't want to assume," I smiled. Nestor took this as the cue to leave. He climbed the stairs to join Mable in the room she'd picked for them.

"We need to put out presents for Winnie," I said.

"I'll go grab them from the truck," he said.

As he went outside, I slipped up the stairs and peeked in on Winnie. Her little snores filled the girly room. I shut the door softly. Pushing power through my tattoo, I brushed the edges of the doorframe placing a protection on the door. As I passed Levi's door, I heard him snoring as well. I placed the same protection on his door. Down the hall a bit, I heard Nestor still moving around in the room. That room received the same protections. Through my fairy eyes, I could see the warm glow around each room. My family. Mine.

Sneaking into the bedroom, I pulled a box I'd masked with

magic out of the bottom of the closet. Tearing off my clothes as fast as I could, I slipped on the red velvet short dress. Long red and white striped stockings rolled up my legs making them look even longer than they were. I slipped on red high heels that would make a drag queen proud. Looking in the mirror, I pulled my hair back as slipped on a red and white hat with a little sprig of mistletoe. The outfit was a perfect mix of slut and Christmas cheer. I laughed at myself trying to be a trailer park queen.

Stalking down the steps without the heels clacking against the wooden steps proved to be a challenge. I watched as Dylan arranged Winnie's presents in front of the Christmas tree which included a bright pink bike that he put together while we cooked earlier.

"Sorry, I had to change," I announced when I got close enough.

He turned to look at me. I put my hands on my hips and lifted my eyebrows at him. He fell back flat on the floor and stared at the ceiling. I heard him muttering something.

"What are you doing?" I laughed at him.

"Thanking every god in every pantheon that you are mine," he smiled up at me. "Is this my Christmas present?"

"Some of it," I replied. "Ho, ho, ho." He reached up and pulled me down on top of him. Tracing my neck with kisses, I felt the warmth of his body pulsing next to mine. He'd always said I felt cool to him. We were complete opposites, but when the elements combined, there were fireworks. Suddenly he stopped.

"This house is full of people. We can't do this here," he said.

"Hmm, well, we could if I put protections on everyone's door that would give us a warning if anyone leaves their room?"

"Oh, you are so good," he said. I took my hat off and put it on his head.

"Merry Christmas, Darlin'," I said.

14

CHRISTMAS DAY

BEFORE THE SUN MADE AN APPEARANCE, I HEARD THE SOFT CHIME OF
bells. "The alarm," I said bolting up in the bed. I still wore the
outfit, minus the shoes. While it's romantic to make love on the
floor in front of a fireplace, once was enough. The damn floor
was hard.

"Winnie?" he asked.

"Yep," I said as he slipped on his jeans. "Put some clothes
on woman!"

Sliding out of the bed, I gathered my shoes from the corner of
the room as Dylan ran downstairs to catch Winnie. I heard a
second chime indicating that Levi was up too. I crossed in front of
the bedroom door making eye contact with Levi.

"Holy shit!" he muttered looking me up and down.

"Git downstairs," I motioned for him to go. His eyes were
locked on me, so I slammed the door. I heard him grunt, then
descend the stairs. I threw on pajama pants and a t-shirt, then
padded downstairs.

"I wanna see!" Winnie whined.

"We were waiting on Aunt Grace," Levi explained.

"Okay, go," I said. She ran into the living room squealing like
Bo, the cake eating troll.

Levi passed me and muttered, "Dylan is damn lucky."

"Thanks, Dublin," I said. He nodded and joined Winnie on the floor with all the toys.

The exchange didn't escape Dylan because he lifted an eyebrow as I approached him. "I walked past the door as he came out of his room," I said.

"Oh, well, every man needs visions of sugarplums for Christmas," he said without a hint of jealousy. "I'll start some coffee."

We watched Winnie play with her new toys. I made breakfast for everyone. Nestor and Mable packed up their things, heading back to town. Some of her family was getting together for lunch, and Nestor was going to meet all of them.

Around noon, I got the call from the med center. It was Tabitha.

"She's gone," she said.

"Thanks for calling, Tabitha. Shouldn't you be at home with your family?" I asked.

"My shift ends in an hour. Merry Christmas, Grace," she said hanging up.

Dylan met my eyes.

"Med center," I replied. Levi turned to look at me when I said the words. They knew from the look in my eyes. I didn't have to speak it for Winnie's sake. I wanted her to enjoy Christmas. We would tell her about her mom later. Levi grabbed her, and she squealed again. He hugged her tight. When she realized that he was hugging, she wrapped her arms around his neck squeezing him back. She quickly went back to playing, but the mood changed in the room.

Dylan refilled his coffee cup. Nestor had given him a giant tin of his special coffee. He offered to refill mine. We leaned next to each other at the bar watching Winnie play. "You okay?" he asked.

"I'm scared," I said.

"All parents are," he said.

"I just want to give her everything she's never had," I said.

He hugged me. "You've already given her the best Christmas she's ever had."

"She doesn't know what's happened," I said as the tears started to flow.

"We will tell her together," he said. "We will do it all together."

Winnie passed out on the couch, so Levi took the Harley for a ride. Dylan and I shared a recliner much like the one in my old trailer. Resting my head against his chest, I listened to his heartbeat.

"Are you going to replace the trailer?" he asked.

"Of course, I've been wanting a bigger one. Levi needs his own bathroom," I said.

"I've never noticed him to be messy," Dylan said.

"It's not the mess. It's the bare-chested parades through the living room," I admitted.

He laughed making my head bounce up and down on his chest. "You aren't jealous?" I asked.

"Grace, who did you buy that kinky little outfit for? Me or Levi?" he asked.

"You know, I bought it for you," I said.

"No, I'm not jealous," he replied. "I was before you gave into me, but not now." I rose up and looked at him.

"Were you?"

"Mainly because he got to be with you all the time," he said.

"He was fucking Kady most of the time," I said.

For a moment, the whole house shuddered. "What the hell?" he asked while leaning the recliner up. The house shook again, only harder this time.

"Can't I just have a happy holiday!?" I screamed waking Winnie. She stared at my outburst. "I'm sorry, honey. Go back to sleep." She plopped her head back down.

"The mother?" Dylan speculated.

We walked out onto the columned front porch and watched a hulking woman march down the drive with a young troll hanging from her left arm. His feet twisted below him as her gait was too long for him to keep up. Behind her the twelve brothers followed hanging their heads.

Dylan shut the door behind us. I hoped that Winnie would be safe. I pushed power through my tattoo. Glittering to life, I traced the door frame placing a protection on the threshold of the house. Nothing supernatural could cross it without an invitation.

"You got a gun?" I asked him.

"Do I have my pants on?" he smirked. Without thinking, I looked at his legs. "Seriously?"

I rolled my eyes at him watching the slow pounding approach of the ogress mother of the thirteen lads. Levi had found very little about her. Other than she was huge and ugly. Both of those facts were confirmed as she stepped beyond the line of oaks.

"Where is the fairy queen?" she spat. Her skin, mottled with brown splotches, had a greenish tone to it. Her teeth were jagged and brown. Her back caused her to hunch forward, but she balanced this way without a cane. A large black cat the size of a mountain lion circled her legs.

I shifted my appearance so that she would not mistake me for a mere human. My hair switched to platinum and lengthened. My eye flicked to a deep turquoise allowing me to see her fairy form. She was covered in festering boils which oozed with green gunk. "My goodness, you fell out of the ugly tree and hit every branch on the way down," I smirked. Dylan coughed behind me. Fuck diplomacy. She was here to pick a fight.

"You puny thing are the daughter of the great King Oberon?" she asked.

"The one and only," I replied.

"Seems he would have taught you manners, but I suppose that's why he kicked you out of his realm," she said knowing more about me than I expected.

I slowly walked down the front steps of the house to stand on the concrete walk that lead to the main drive. "What do you want?"

She tossed poor Taylor toward me, and his body rolled into a heap between us. "My son wants to marry you," she said. I saw the steady rise and fall of his chest. Thankfully, he was still alive.

"I belong to Mr. Dylan Riggs," I said pointing behind me.

She snarled at him. "I've come a long way to see my son married to you. He brought his brothers here, and they've helped him prepare for a wonderful ceremony and feast. You will marry him."

"This is *my* town. You don't get to come here to order me around," I spouted at her. "In fact, I've had just about enough of fairy and magic bullshit this season. Your sons are a collected menace to society. Take them and leave," I warned her.

"Or what will you do little Queen?" she asked.

Unleashing power pent up in my stirring emotions, the grass frosted over and climbed the large oaks down the lane. The sky darkened as snow started to fall. I stalked slowly toward her, one icy step at a time. "Leave now," I said.

Her sons cowered behind her. I wasn't sure if they were more afraid of me or her. "I will leave if you negotiate a trade," she said.

"Speak your terms," I allowed it.

"I smell a small child," she purred as she ran a long black finger-nail across her tongue. "So young and juicy."

My anger boiled over as I raised a hand to blast her with ice. Unleashing the power, it hit her solid, but she didn't freeze. It bounced off of her. "Fuck," I muttered.

She cackled as she circled a bony finger in the air. A trail of light followed her as I felt power being drawn from the surrounding area. I cringed knowing that I would have to pull power from the oaks to have enough to make a dent in her. I circled her to the right as she continued to trace the air between us. I stepped over the limp form of Taylor to reach the first tree. Keeping an eye on her, I spoke to the tree instructing it to funnel power to me. The ancient tree acknowledged me as the tattoo on my arm pulsed with a humming pulse.

The power that the tree pulled was old and strong. It knew what I needed to disable if not kill the ogress.

"Grace," Dylan warned as the woman stopped drawing.

"Guard that door. Don't let her take my child," I replied. He nodded as his eyes flared with blue flame.

"Oh, the Phoenix. No wonder you don't want my boy," she laughed. "He has power, but neither of you have enough to defeat me."

Her eyes twitched behind me to my left. I dared to glance over my shoulder to see a blue-jean clad bard carrying a guitar approach. "Oh, a bard. Lovely. Play me a little jig," she laughed.

"Stay back, Levi," I said. If he were going to get into the fight, he could play music outside of her reach. I didn't know what he had planned, but I hoped it would help.

Low howls ripped through the air, and two large wolves bounded up the lane behind the lads. They huddled together as the wolves bared their teeth. "And wolves. They are tasty. Picking fur out of your teeth is a bitch though," she laughed.

"Especially when you could eat corn on a cob through a picket fence," I taunted her.

"Momma, maybe we should just go," Lamar suggested.

"Don't doubt your momma," she warned him. He nodded hobbling back into the huddle of trolls.

A loud voice bellowed behind her, "Gryla, there is only room in this town for one flesh eater."

She slowly turned to face the hulking goat form of Krampus. "My esteemed goat-lord," she bowed to him. "I have a grievance with the Queen here. She's shunned my offspring by caging them. She refused the hand of my youngest. She has slighted us all."

"Your children wreaked havoc in this town. I'd say she's been tolerant. Instead of killing them, she allowed them to live," he said. "You will leave. She protects us. We protect her."

"Interesting. I'd known that your influence grew, however I did not realize you had a following," she smirked as she began to realize that she wasn't going to win this fight. "Come with me boys. Gather your brother. We will leave this hell hole."

"We aren't leaving," Lamar said. "The queen said if we straightened up our acts, that we could stay."

"You will go with me," she spouted while the black cat hissed.

A harsh strum across strings broke through the sounds of the cat's challenge. The cat couched batting its ears with its paws. Gryla spun towards Levi flinging white lightning toward his position. I turned to motion at the ground between us. A large ice wall appeared to block the lightning.

She let out a disgusted howl flinging lightning toward the wolves. They bounced away into the woods, but their low growls continued to be heard. Krampus advanced on her. She did not miss. The lightning struck him in the chest flinging him across the field. His body laid limp.

Alternating hands, I pushed my ice block spell toward her over and over. It bounced off with no effect. The brothers scampered over to Taylor and dragged him behind the ice wall with Levi.

She met my throws with lightning. I started to tire, but I didn't know what else I could do.

A clap of thunder rippled through the air. I turned to face Dylan whose body flickered with flames. He slowly approached her. Each step he took, thunder rolled over the farm. The snow intensified with my rising emotions. She flashed lightning toward Dylan, but his flame consumed it causing him to burn brighter. As I stared at him, I realized that if I didn't know the man behind the fire, he'd scare the shit out of me. Snow, ice, thunder and lightning in a perfect storm.

"You will leave," he demanded. "The Queen has ordered it."

"Dear Phoenix, this fight does not have to involve you," she said backing away from him.

Large flaming wings extended outward from his back. She stumbled backwards into a heap. He stopped advancing. The radiating heat around him throbbed, and I took several steps back from him. The last thing I needed was the Ice Queen to be subdued by her own boyfriend. At least, not in front of an enemy.

"Leave!" he bellowed.

"My sons," she cried out clutching the large cat to her chest. She flicked her eyes to the ice wall where her sons were hiding.

Dylan locked her gaze. "Leave or die," he stated.

"Damn, that's hot," I said. He smiled beneath the flame.

"This isn't over," she sputtered. But I knew it was. We didn't even have to strike at her. She cowered away. The last of her lightning formed a circle around her. She spoke a few words and vanished.

Flaming Dylan turned to me. I took a long look at his wonderfully naked body, that I couldn't touch, but enjoyed the sight for the moment before he sprinted to the house as the flame extinguished.

The ice wall cracked and fell. Taylor was sitting up with a bit of blood trickling out of his mouth. I reached and lightly touched it. It healed.

"I'm never washing my lips again," he sighed.

"He's got it bad, my Queen," Phil said.

"We are sorry for all the trouble we caused," Ryan added.

"Could we please stay?" Cory asked.

"We would swear not to cause trouble," Willie offered.

I paced for a moment as Dylan emerged from the house with Winnie. "Snow!" she squealed running out into it. She ran in circles as it fell from the darkened sky. She stopped when she saw Phil. The troll who took her milk.

"They won't hurt you, Winnie," I assured her.

"Okay, Elsa," she said. Levi died laughing.

"Hush your mouth, Levi, and go check on Deacon." I pointed at him. The trolls laughed too. "All of you!"

Several "Yes, ma'ams" came from the group while Levi sprinted into the field. I heard the howl of wolves which told me that Amanda and Troy were returning to their home.

"I'm just Aunt Grace," I said bending down in front of her. Her small hand touched my face.

She giggled when she realized how cold my skin was. "You have sparkles on your face," she said. The normal fairy luminescence was amplified by my cold exterior.

I went and sat down on the steps of Dylan's house. He took a seat next to me, and the ice queen melted. Winnie ran up to us, standing with Dylan. I supposed she wasn't so sure about me changing costumes in front of her. I'd think of some way to explain it to her. Perhaps I was her fairy godmother in disguise.

Exhausted, I beckoned the trolls to approach. They stood around waiting for my permission to stay in Shady Grove.

"You have to make up for the things you've done," I said. They looked at each other than formed a little huddle to discuss amongst themselves.

Finally, they turned around facing me with large grins. Lamar stepped forward toward Winnie. He cupped his hands and shook them. Lifting his top hand from his bottom hand, a small wooden carving of a unicorn sat in his hand. He offered it to her. She looked at me for permission, so I nodded. "Thank you," she muttered.

Phil approached her. She watched him pull a copper cup out of his pocket. "Little miss, milk is best in a metal cup. It stays cold." He offered her the cup, and she gladly took it.

"Thank you," she smiled.

Eric, the bed pan troll, stepped forward, producing a metal chain with a W charm hanging from it. He offered, she received and thanked him. The gift giving continued with each troll.

Cory offered her a small spoon with a long handle. He

informed her it was for ice cream sundaes for which Chad, the bowl thief gave her a tall sundae glass.

Willie, the leftover troll, gave her a small container with dividers. He told her that she could keep anything in it she wanted, but it was perfect for separating leftovers.

Phillip, the bane of Brad the BBQ man, handed her what looked to be a miniature sausage extruder. He pulled the knob back and instructed her to push it back in. As she did, the warbling song of a bird. She pulled it in and out several times giggling with each whistle.

Richard, the peeping Dick, presented her with a small pair of binoculars. She put them to her eyes and stared at us all up close.

Bo, the nosey cake-eater, offered her a beautiful red velvet cupcake with green sprinkles. She danced with excitement. She'd started handing gifts off to Dylan and me as she anticipated the next one.

The truck destroyer, Ryan, offered her a die cast red Camaro just like Dylan's. I laughed, because I knew she loved his car.

Sweet, lovestruck Taylor approached. "She's like a mini-you," he said to me.

"Don't get any ideas," Dylan said.

"No, of course not," he said. He pulled out a red rose made of pure crystal. She squealed.

"Oh, so pretty," she cooed. He handed it to her and slowly backed away.

"My queen, each year, my brothers and I will make amends by presenting the children of Shady Grove with toys, if they are good," Lamar said.

"All of you?" I asked. Lamar nodded. "Hey, what about you, Door Slammer?"

Keith stood in the back with his hands in his pockets. He snarled, stepping forward. Reaching in his pocket, he revealed a golden key. He handed it to her. "This key is special, Winnie. It opens the door to heaven. So, if you are ever sad or missing someone who no longer lives here with us. You can hold your key while thinking about the person, and they will look down from heaven and see you." He shoved his hands in his pants pockets and backed into the crowd of brothers.

I had to wipe the tears from my cheeks as Dylan put his arm around me. "I don't know anyone in heaven," she said clasping the key.

"Winnie, come here," I said. She stood before me holding her little key. "Your momma is in heaven now with the angels. So, let's hold your key together and think about her." Little tears formed in the corners of her eyes, but she offered me the key. I wrapped my hands around hers. Dylan put his warm hand over both of ours. I hadn't realized that Levi had made it back from the field, but he put his hand under all of them.

"Can she see me?" she asked.

"Of course, she can. She's smiling at you. You got so many new presents, and she wants you to be happy," I said choking the last words out.

The trolls sniffed. Ryan produced a hanky blowing his nose loudly as Lamar elbowed him in the ribs. They all cried, except Keith who watched the ground at his feet.

"Who is my mommy now?" she asked.

"If it's okay with you, I want you to stay with me," I said. She nodded as we all released her hands. She wrapped her arms around my neck and hugged me. "I promise I'll take good care of you."

"I know," she muttered. "As long as Uncle Levi can still be my Uncle. And Mr. Dylan can be my Mister."

"I think that would be fine," I replied.

"Absolutely," Levi said. Dylan smiled at her and kissed her on the forehead.

"Thank you all," I said to the trolls. "I look forward to the thirteen days of Christmas next year."

They smiled and wiped away tears. Turning to walk back down

the lane, they caught up with Krampus who offered them all a place to stay in his barn until they found proper homes around the exotic fairy city of Shady Grove, AL.

That evening Remington Blake called to wish us all a Merry Christmas. The hospital had contacted him about Bethany's death. He asked me if I wanted to handle the funeral expenses. I told him that I did. I wanted it to be simple though for Winnie's sake. He agreed to take care of the details for me, and that the paperwork giving me full custody would be filed with the state right after the holiday.

Levi put Winnie to bed. I asked him if he had plans to see Kady, and he said no. That they were still dating, but needed to see less of each other which made absolutely no sense to me. However, I needed to stay neutral when it came to his love life. No more assaults on girlfriends. Unless they deserved it, of course.

Dylan and I curled up on the couch watching the fire and the lights on the tree twinkling.

"It's over," he said.

"Heavens to Betsy, it better be," I laughed. "You were impressive, Mr. Fire Bird."

"She was frightened of me. I think it was mostly a show of strength. She knew she couldn't take us all," he said.

"It was you," I reinforced.

He nuzzled my cheek. "I want you to stay. Give Levi the trailer when you get a new one. Keep a room there if it makes you feel better, but I want you here with me."

"I don't think it matters whether I call that home or not. I will be with you wherever you are," I assured him.

"I love you, Grace," he said. "Beautiful Grace."

"I love you, too." I reached under the couch, pulling out a wrapped box.

"You already gave me a Christmas present," he smiled.

"Yeah, but you can't show that one off. This one, you can," I said.

Untying the ribbon, he carefully pulled the paper off. He smiled at the wooden box with the name D. Riggs carved in the top.

"Open it," I prodded.

"Okay, okay," he said as he clicked the latch. Opening the lid, he found two engraved 1911 Kimber pistols. One was intricately tooled with flames running down the barrel and a fiery winged bird on the wooden grip. The other had Native American geometric shapes along the barrel with a traditional thunderbird carved into the wooden grip. He stared at them as he ran his fingers over the tooling.

"Well?" I asked.

"Grace, these are amazing. Where in the world did you find someone to do this?" he asked.

I reached in and flipped them over. D. Riggs was tooled into the other side of each barrel. He shook his head in amazement. "I know a guy," I smiled.

He closed the box and laid it on the floor as he pulled my face to his. "I'm blown away. They are perfect. I had to give my favorite guns back to the department when I left. These are amazing."

"I knew you had to give them back. Troy told me. Plus, if you are going to be a private investigator, you will need them," I said.

"Nestor said you were worried about that," he said.

"Nestor needs to keep our conversations private," I laughed. "I just don't want lose you."

"I'm not going anywhere," he said as he kissed me again. "I don't want you running off on me."

"What? I'm not leaving," I said.

"You've said several times that this Queen thing was more than you anticipated. Part of me wonders if you will run eventually," he said truthfully.

"I promise. I couldn't leave you. If I leave, I'm taking you with me," I laughed.

"I certainly hope so," he said with a strange look in his eye.

"What's wrong?" He pushed me up off of him, grabbing the gun box. He headed to the stairs.

"Dylan?" He ignored me practically stomping away.

I followed him. He opened a small door in the hallway that I thought was an electrical box, but it was a safe. He punched in a code, the placed his thumb on a pad. The safe popped open, and he slipped the guns inside. He shut the door back, locking the safe. His right hand twitched inside his pocket.

"Grace, let's go to bed. It's been a long day," he said turning toward the bedroom. I grabbed his arm and pulled. "What are you doing?"

Levi came out of his room. "What's going on?"

"I guess we haven't fought in a while, and Dylan felt like it was time," I said.

"Levi, go back to bed," Dylan growled.

"Dude, chill out," Levi said as he went back into his room. I felt his presence close to the door. My bard worried about me.

"I don't want to fight," he said as he pulled his hand out of his pocket. I saw what I knew he had. A small velvet box.

Looking at him, then down at the box, I realized that he had cold feet. His last relationship caused him a lot of anxiety about asking her to marry him. I approached him slowly. "I don't want to fight either," I said. "But if you don't give me my Christmas present, I'm gonna be pissed."

He smirked. "So pushy."

"It's almost fitting that we pretend to fight during this, right?" I asked trying to make him calm down.

"No."

Sigh. "Put it back in your pocket," I said. "I'll pretend I didn't see it."

He spun and stalked to the bedroom. I followed in behind him.

Once both feet were in the room, the door slammed behind me. He was pressed against me in a moment. His forehead leaning down to touch mine. "You weren't the only one that used to be afraid," he said.

"I know that," I said.

"Would you shut up?" I laughed, but nodded. "I knew I wanted you. I knew I wanted us, but the fear was actually getting to this point. Getting over the past. Accepting what we have."

He kissed me on the cheek. The hand holding the box met mine. Pressing the box between our hands, I felt the soft cover on it as he clamped down on my hand to prevent me from opening it.

"And now?"

"Now, I just want you to have everything, and it be perfect. But I let my nerves get the best of me. Now, we are standing here like fools talking instead of making love."

"Skip the box, then," I suggested.

"You would really do that?" he asked.

"Lord knows I've tortured you. You might as well torture me," I said. For a moment, I looked into his eyes. He really wasn't going to show me what was in the box. He was going to chicken out. I tightened my fingers around the box, yanking it as hard as I could. He laughed, but I had his hand too with the box.

"Stop, Grace, stop," he ordered me.

I paused. "I'm waiting?" I said.

"For what?"

"Show me the fucking box," I said.

"Vulgar mouth," he muttered as his lips met mine. I kissed him back tracing his lips with my tongue. I felt his hand loosen, and I jerked again. "Good try."

"You aren't nervous. You are a damn tease, Dylan Riggs," I shouted.

"Stop, you'll wake up Winnie," he laughed.

I tried just yanking my hand away from his without the box, but that didn't work either. "Shit or get off the pot, Dylan Riggs!"

"Yes, ma'am," he said as he sank to his knee.

"Oh, shit," I muttered. He laughed.

"Will you marry me?" he asked, blue eyes shining.

I looked down at his hand and nodded toward the box. He shook his head. "What?!"

"Answer me. Grace Ann Bryant, will you marry me?"

"Yes, now show..." he was up again with his mouth on mine pulling me toward the bed. When we reached the edge, he sat down on it and opened the box.

"You devil," I said. The logo on the inside of the box was the same as the logo on the inside of the pistols I gave him. He knew a guy, too. Much like the guns, the sides of the band of the ring were tooled. One side with delicate snowflakes, the other with flames. The center stone was a heart shaped diamond with a flanking ruby and sapphire. As I stared it, a lump grew in my chest pressing down on my lungs.

"Say something," he whispered in my ear.

"I will when I can breathe again," I said as he removed it from the box. He slipped it on my finger, but kept his eyes on mine.

"Better than the one Levi gave you?" he asked. I'd completely forgotten my fake engagement to Levi, but he hadn't.

I laughed expelling the air I'd held in my lungs. "I, um, what?" I lost my train of thought staring at it.

"Tongue tied?" he asked.

"No, you just got my tinsel in a tangle," I laughed.

ACKNOWLEDGMENTS

I knew I wanted to write a Christmas story for Grace and crew as soon as I finished the first book. I enjoyed writing her story so much that I debated on writing a Christmas short for my Path to Redemption series or to write a Christmas book. Timing was definitely an issue, but as soon as I started writing Tinsel in a Tangle, I knew that it didn't matter when I finished it that it would be so much fun to read.

As I researched Christmas traditions and mythology, I came across the story of the 13 Yule Lads. I debated on tackling such a vast story considering that I wanted to adapt it to modern day. In the legends, the Yule Lads do forsake their mischievous ways and bring presents to Icelandic children for thirteen days leading up to Christmas.

The challenge also was to name all of these characters. I decided to pattern them after my co-workers who have been extremely supportive. So, when you read about the trolls, they are my fellow workers at my "other" job.

Thank you to Lamar, Phil, Cory, Willie, Chad, Keithon, Kevin, Phillip, Richard, Bo, Ryan, Chris (Taylor), Jessica, Sharolyn, Tonya, Brad and Tabitha. I've always written my books with keen awareness to the meanings and origins of names. In this book, the origins are simple. They are the people I see daily who challenge me. Thank you all.

From early in life Kimbra Swain was indoctrinated in the ways of geekdom. Raised on Star Wars, Tolkien, Superheroes and Voltron, she found herself immersed in a world of imagination. She started writing in high school, and completed her English degree from the University of Alabama in 2003.

Her writing is influenced by a gamut of favorite authors including Jane Austen, J.R.R. Tolkien, L.M. Montgomery, Timothy Zahn, Kathy Reichs, Kevin Hearne and Jim Butcher.

Born and raised in Alabama, Kimbra still lives there with her husband and 5-year-old daughter. When she isn't reading or writing, she plays PC games, makes jewelry and builds cars.

Kimbra is currently writing Reincarnation, Book 3 of the Path to Redemption Series to be released in February, as well as two historical novellas for that series, Deception and Devotion.

Grace and company will return in January. The book, which doesn't have a title yet, will focus on the new fairy council elections. If you think humans have wild elections, just wait until they are Shady Grove style.

Follow Kimbra on Facebook, Twitter,
Instagram, Pinterest, and GoodReads.
www.kimbraswain.com

facebook.com/kimbraswainofficial

twitter.com/kswainauthor

instagram.com/kswainauthor

pinterest.com/kimbraswain

goodreads.com/Kimbra_Swain

28795859R00127

Made in the USA
San Bernardino, CA
09 March 2019